THE NUDE
a new perspective

Since Kenneth Clark's major study, *The Nude*, appeared in 1956, value changes and social changes (influenced particularly by the rise of feminism), as well as aesthetic and technological developments in painting and photography, have produced new attitudes to the role and meaning of the naked body in art. This book surveys what has always been an emotive and contentious subject, from the perspective of the 80s. It shows, through a wide range of illustrations, how the attitudes of artists and public have changed throughout history, from classical Greece to the present day. Chapters include: Historical Context; Drawing the Nude; Active Versus Passive; The Fetishized Female; Nature Versus Culture; New Directions?

Gill Saunders has been a curator in the Department of Designs, Prints and Drawings at the Victoria & Albert Museum since 1980. She has written on a variety of art historical subjects; her particular interests are women artists and images of women in art.

GILL SAUNDERS

THE NUDE

a new perspective

ICON EDITIONS

HARPER & ROW, PUBLISHERS
Cambridge, Philadelphia, San Francisco, London,
Mexico City, São Paulo, Singapore, Sydney

1817

FIRST U.S. EDITION
Library of Congress Catalog Card Number: 89-45113

ISBN 0–06–438508–6
ISBN 0–06–430189–3 (pbk.)

89 90 91 92 93   10 9 8 7 6 5 4 3 2 1

Printed and bound by Jolly & Barber Ltd, Rugby, Warwickshire, England

FRONTISPIECE: Untitled image from *Minotaure* 1933, by Brassai (see p.100).

CONTENTS

ACKNOWLEDGEMENTS   6

INTRODUCTION   7

HISTORICAL CONTEXT   9

DRAWING THE NUDE   17

ACTIVE VERSUS PASSIVE   21

THE FETISHIZED FEMALE   71

NATURE VERSUS CULTURE   91

NEW DIRECTIONS?   116

NOTES   140

BIBLIOGRAPHY   141

INDEX OF ARTISTS   143

ACKNOWLEDGEMENTS

This book would not have been possible without the ideas, advice, knowledge and criticism of many friends and colleagues. In particular I must thank John Murdoch for the suggestion from which this project grew, and for his support and encouragement throughout; Chris Titterington who generously shared his ideas in many conversations and offered trenchant criticism at all stages; Robert Sharp who kindly read the final draft and saved me from many errors of fact and infelicities of expression; Philip Spruyt de Bay for the excellent photographs of V & A material; and my indefatigable editor Julia MacKenzie, who has been unfailingly supportive, patient and good humoured in trying circumstances.

Finally, I must acknowledge a huge debt to all those whose researches I have drawn on in the writing of this book, and thank all those artists and dealers who generously contributed information and illustrations at very short notice.

INTRODUCTION

Significance is inherent in the human body.
Julia Kristeva, *Desire in Language* (1980)

Nudity is a politically, socially and sexually 'loaded' subject, liable to provoke extreme responses. There can be no doubt that the female body is used excessively and indiscriminately in our visual culture (see newspaper, magazine and billboard advertising for examples) but certain feminists and other censorious pressure groups react to such images with a similar lack of discrimination, condemning all as exploiting and degrading women or as outraging public morals. With regard to context and content, of course, women may enjoy images of the nude as much as men. However, it must be said that there is an imbalance between the sexes, for the male nude is seen much less often either in fine art or in other visual media. The violent reactions provoked by the exhibition 'Women's Images of Men' at the Institute of Contemporary Arts, London, in 1982 suggest that men are equally threatened, psychically if not physically, by images of themselves naked. The problems that we have with images of the male nude, and their relative invisibility in our culture can be explained largely by the nature of nudity as perceived in this society. 'Nude' is synonymous with 'female nude' because nakedness connotes passivity, vulnerability; it is powerless and anonymous. In other words it is a 'female' state and equated with femininity. In Rubens's *Cain Slaying Abel*, Abel the victim is naked, his assailant clad in an animal skin. This nakedness is both a sign of his status as victim, and at the same time one of the factors which render him physically vulnerable.

Emotive and contentious, the naked body in art is the focus for a variety of meanings. Since the formal and aesthetic aspects of the nude have been exhaustively studied, the aim of this book is to look at those meanings, with particular reference to the differences in presentation and function between the male and female nude. The final section will discuss the revival and redirection of the nude in feminist art today.

DIANE ARBUS (1927–71)
Two Nudists 1963
Gelatin silver print

Arbus was obsessed with freaks, a fact her two middle-aged naturist subjects seem to sense as they face the camera, trying to appear relaxed but obviously apprehensive. Their nakedness renders them vulnerable to the intrusive gaze of the camera.

The two spreading and ageing bodies seem pitiful to us, uncomfortably out-of-context because they do not conform to the usual public image of nudity – young, perfect, almost exclusively female. Significantly, such an image, a sultry and pneumatic fifties starlet, hangs on the wall behind them. Thus we have nudity in its publicly sanctioned form, provocative, passive, sexually desirable, contrasted with nudity as it is, imperfect, shaming and shameful, private made shockingly public.

HISTORICAL CONTEXT

The nude is indelibly a term of art and art criticism: the
fact is that art criticism and sexual discourse intersect
at this point, and the one provides the other with crucial
representations, forms of knowledge and standards of
decorum.

T.J. Clark, *Preliminaries to a Possible Treatment
of 'Olympia' in 1865* (1982)[1]

Our culture is built, in part, on two contradictory philosophies whose
conflicting ideas are clearly evident in the attitude to the naked
human body. For the Greeks, the nude, apart from its celebration
of physical beauty, expressed the nobility and potential of the human spirit,
but in Christian theology nakedness became a symbol of shame and guilt;
the gestures which imply nothing more than modesty in the *Venus Pudica*
become signs of sinfulness, grief and humiliation in Masaccio's *Eve driven
from Paradise*. A shameful awareness of their nakedness is the first reaction
of Adam and Eve after eating the fruit of the tree of knowledge: 'And the
eyes of them both were opened and they knew that they were naked; and
they sewed leaves together and made themselves aprons. And the Lord God
called unto the man and said unto him "Where art thou?" And he said "I
heard thy voice in the garden, and I was afraid, because I was naked; and I
hid myself." ' (Genesis 3: 7, 9, 10.)

In the Christian art of the Gothic period (twelfth to sixteenth centuries)
the naked figure is found only in representations of the Last Judgement and
the torments of Hell. The moral is obvious – nakedness is the outward sign
of the sins of the flesh indulged and will be punished accordingly. The
medieval theologians defined four symbolic types of nudity: *nuditas naturalis*,
the natural state of man as born into the world, the state of innocence
represented by Adam and Eve before the Fall; *nuditas temporalis*, the volun-
tary lack of worldly goods, as represented by St Francis, stripping publicly
to renounce the world and embrace his spiritual vocation; *nuditas virtualis*, a
state of nakedness intended to symbolize innocence, purity, truth; *nuditas
criminalis*, symbolic of lust, vanity and self-indulgent sin. The Gothic disgust
with the naked body, especially the female body, is summed up by St John

Chrysostom in his warning to 'The Fallen Monk Theodore' against the outward fairness of women: 'The whole of her bodily beauty is nothing less than phlegm, blood and bile, rheum and the fluid of digested food. . . Are you then in a flutter of excitement about the storehouse of these things?' The Renaissance nude, by contrast, demonstrates a reversion to classical ideals and precedents. Man's nobility and potential for perfection were embodied in the naked figure. Vitruvian architectural theory advocated buildings scaled to the proportions of a man, and Leonardo da Vinci drew the most successful of the many attempts to prove that the (male) body was the pattern for those perfect geometric shapes, the circle and the square. As an image of perfection the naked body was used to symbolize ideal concepts such as Truth (Botticelli) or Sacred Love (Titian).

Thus is the naked body in art ambiguous, and nudity subject to conflicting interpretations – in Christian philosophy it can connote sin, guilt and shame, with the female body personifying sexual temptation, as we see not only from Eve, but also the stories of Susannah and Bathsheba; in classical philosophy nudity is not criminal, though the female nude is nevertheless a symbol of sexuality. The nude has remained constant as a subject of art in all ages of European society, whatever the prevailing attitude to the public display of the body. Objections to the fact of nudity are rare; it is only the character or presentation of that nudity which attracts criticism. Thus Queen Victoria, usually a symbol of her era's alleged prudishness, happily purchased a Mulready life-drawing as a gift for Prince Albert, but contemporary critics attacked his, Frost's and Etty's painted nudes because they were too plainly the bodies of lower-class women, with unperfected proportions and the marks of the corsets still upon them.[2] Etty was castigated by *The Times* for presenting his models 'in the most gross and literal manner' rather than aiming for the 'exquisite idealities' of Titian. In our time the female nude is generally acceptable but the male nude can still provoke censorship: in 1977 Wheelock College in Boston banned a display of images of male nudes (female nudes remained on exhibition) and certain distributors of *Ms* magazine refused to handle it for some months after it ran a feature reproducing a series of paintings of naked men. In 1988 the British edition of *Elle* magazine carried a letter from a mother outraged by the publication of a picture by Lucian Freud featuring a nude man, on the grounds that it was unsuitable viewing for her teenage daughter; she made no mention of the female nudes so frequently featured in fashion shots, health and beauty articles, and advertisements in the same magazine. And in November 1988 the *Sun*, a newspaper noted for its Page 3 photographs of half-naked girls and a high quota of salacious sex stories, carried on its front page a self-righteous account of a male nude being censored. The painting, which showed a naked boy with an erection, formed part of an exhibition called 'The Invisible Male: The Construction of Male Identity'; it was deemed an affront to the sensibilities of the Princess Royal and the gallery was consequently crossed off the proposed royal itinerary.

GREEK (HELLENISTIC)
Venus de Medici
Marble
(Uffizi Gallery, Florence)

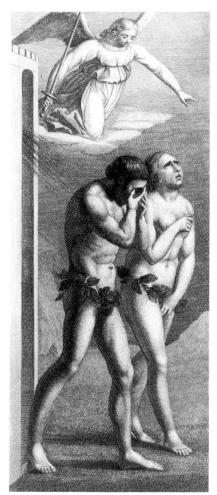

AFTER MASACCIO (1401–?28)
*The Expulsion: Adam and Eve driven
from Paradise* (after the fresco in the
Brancacci Chapel, Florence)
Engraving

The Fall was precipitated by woman's
sexuality; it is appropriate therefore that
Eve alone should conceal her genitals,
while Adam shields his face and his eyes
from the sight that tempted him to sin.

Front page of the *Sun*, 3 November 1988

PETER PAUL RUBENS (1577–1640)
Cain Slaying Abel
Oil on canvas
(Courtauld Institute Galleries, London
(Princes Gate Collection))

STEFANO DE GIOVANNI SASSETTA
(*c.*1400, perhaps 1392–1450)
St Francis renounces his earthly father
(detail)
Oil on panel
(The National Gallery, London)

ANONYMOUS: SWISS SCHOOL 1473
The Martyrdom of Saint Agatha
(part of an altarpiece)
Oil on panel
(Courtesy of Silvano Lodi)

Images of the naked body are rare in the art of the late Gothic period, and the female nude with its inflammatory power especially so. This, however, was an acceptable portrayal of female nudity, for it shows the body (and specifically the breasts, emblem of femaleness) being mutilated, punished for the temptations it offers to men. Many stories of female martyrdom include scenes in which the victim is stripped naked as part of the process of degradation, but described by male commentators in lascivious terms.

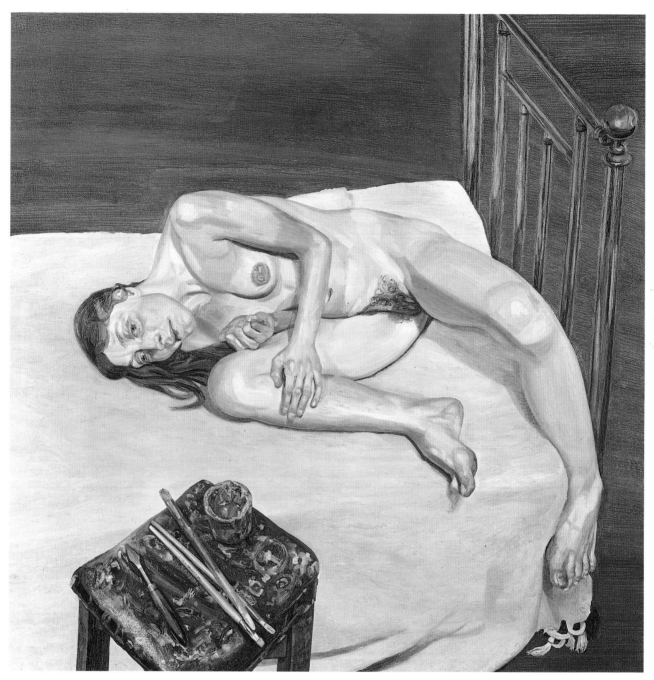

LUCIAN FREUD (b.1922)
Naked Portrait 1972–3
Oil on canvas
(The Tate Gallery, London)

Freud's nudes, male and female, are always recognizably portraits, though anonymously so. Despite this, Freud renders the body dispassionately, arranging it like a still life. The woman is poised between display and concealment, one leg drawn up to her chest as she curls into the foetal position, the other painfully stretched over the end of the bed and thereby revealing her sex. Her anguished face and the clenched right hand attest to conflicting imperatives.

DRAWING THE NUDE

The male nude has been the basis of art training from the fifteenth century almost to the present day. The study of the nude was largely a means of learning anatomy and establishing a sound basis for the clothed figure. Alberti, in *De Pictura*, explains: 'Before dressing a man we first draw him nude, then we enfold him in draperies. So in painting the nude we place first his bones and muscles which we then cover with flesh so that it is not difficult to understand where each muscle is beneath.' The Academies of Britain and France, established in the eighteenth century, were founded on Renaissance practice. A painter's apprenticeship began with the study and copying of antique originals and casts. Many famous antique figures were rediscovered in the Renaissance period – the Laocoon group, the *Apollo Belvedere*, the Belvedere torso, the *Medici Venus* – and remained an influential part of academic training well into the eighteenth century when we find teachers and theorists such as Joshua Reynolds and Benjamin West extolling their virtues as exemplars to the student. The apprentice painter was only permitted to advance to the next stage of his training – drawing from the living model, naked or draped – when his imagination was well-stocked with ideal forms to counterbalance the distressing variety of nature in the individual. The life model was himself often posed after an antique figure. The male nude was the main subject of academic study until the late eighteenth and early nineteenth century. There were a number of reasons for this, the first being that the male represented physical perfection and that woman was necessarily physically, as well as morally inferior. Studios and academies were a male preserve which excluded women in any capacity, student or model. The sexual puritanism of the Christian tradition also militated against the study of the female life model – even in the later nineteenth century at the Royal Academy Schools the access of the male artists to the female model was strictly controlled, with students under twenty not admitted unless married. Renaissance classicism was itself coloured by its Christian context, and as a consequence female nudes in the painting and sculpture of the period were derived from male models. As a result of this practice they appear unconvincing, either muscular like Michelangelo's figures of *Night* and *Dawn* on the Medici tomb, or androgynous as in the *Venus* by Parentino.

All the theorists, from Vasari to Reynolds, insisted that the creation of an idealized human form must be grounded in a close and exact study of individual models. Though imitation of observed reality was an essential skill, Vasari reserved his highest praise for art which transcended the flawed reality of the model on which it was based: 'The painter becomes a slave if he has to keep a nude or draped model in front of him all the time he is working.' Reynolds quotes Cicero on Phidias with approval: 'Neither did this artist when he carved the image of Jupiter and Minerva, set before him any one human figure, as a pattern, which he was to copy; but having a more perfect idea of beauty fixed in his mind, this he steadily contemplated, and to the imitation of all this his skill and labour were directed.' (*Discourse* III, pp.42–3) but earlier (*Discourse* I, pp.19–20) had advocated 'a habit of exactness and precision' which would advance the artist's knowledge of the human figure. He insisted that idealization of the model can only develop from 'an attentive and well compared study of the human form'. The search for the ideal led to the devising of various theories of human proportions. The Greek nude was constructed according to strict mathematical rules; books such as Audran's *Proportions* attempted to analyse and decipher these systems, while later artists such as Mulready experimented to establish their own.

FREDERICK BLOEMAERT (*c.*1610–*c.*1669)
A Sculptor's Studio
Chiaroscuro wood-engraving with
etched line

The artist's first introduction to
anatomy came through the study of
sculpture and casts. By copying
antique exemplars, he absorbed an idea
of the physical ideal as embodied in the
art of classical cultures.

HENDRIK GOLTZIUS (1558–1617)
An artist sketching the *Apollo Belvedere*
1617
Engraving

BERNARDO PARENTINO (1437–1531)
Venus and Cupid
Pen and ink on vellum

SCHOOL OF PERINO DEL VAGA (1501–47)
Venus and Cupid
Pen, ink and wash

JACOPO TINTORETTO (1518–94)
Seated male nude
Black chalk, squared in charcoal

The female nude model did not exist in the early Renaissance period, largely because the male body was seen as the ideal of perfection from which the female deviated. Consequently, in compositions where the naked female figure was essential, as in these two studies of Venus and Cupid, the artist simply adapts his knowledge of the male physique to create an ill-founded conception of the female body.

Parentino's Venus (p.19) has the androgynous form of a youth; the only concessions to femaleness being the addition of small breasts to the smooth flat torso, and a head of curly tresses. The Venus from the School of Del Vaga is of a massive and muscular build, closely related to Michelangelo's figures, *Night* and *Dawn*, on the Medici tomb.

The male nude in Tintoretto's sketch is found translated as the female in the right foreground of his painting *The Last Supper* (in the Scuola di San Rocco, Venice).

ACTIVE VERSUS PASSIVE

Since the period of the ancient Greeks, the nude as a subject of art has been an obvious site for the construction of sexual difference. Recent research (by John Money and Anke Ehrhardt[3]) has suggested that cultural and social training are far more influential than hormone action in shaping the sexual orientation and behaviour of girls and boys after birth. Attitudes to gender and sexuality enshrined in the essentially patriarchal societies in the West are reflected in representations of the male and female nude. Patriarchal tradition defines sexuality in terms of opposites – domination/submission, active/passive – characterizing men as aggressive, independent and analytical, and women as emotional, nurturing and intuitive. This polarization of gender roles is first formulated in Aristotle, a logical consequence of Greek misogyny: 'Man is active, full of movement, creative in politics, business and culture. The male shapes and moulds society and the world. Woman, on the other hand, is passive. She stays at home as is her nature. She is matter waiting to be formed and moulded by the active male principle.' It is found again in Genesis 3:16 where God admonishes Eve for her sin, telling her 'and thy desire shall be to thy husband and he shall rule over thee'. Society utilizes a variety of verbal and visual strategies to promote these stereotypes, attacking as 'unnatural' those individuals who do not fit. Like any other cultural production, art serves to construct and identify the stereotypes. Images of the nude in art (often possessing an iconic familiarity and power) are as much a part of this process as advertising or media imagery. Previous literature on the nude in art has accepted these categories unquestioningly; in Kenneth Clark's *The Nude* (1956) the male nude is discussed in chapters entitled 'Apollo' and 'Energy', while the female nude is defined exclusively by her sexuality under the headings 'Venus I and II' and 'Ecstasy'.

(i)   Passivity as an attribute of women was an imposition of Western Christian society which sought to control women's sexuality, and by such means maintain and extend the patriarchy. To this end passivity in women was characterized as 'good', activity or autonomy as 'bad'. The Roman writer Lucretius expressed a commonly-held belief that movement by the woman during intercourse would hamper or prevent conception; thus the good wife is passive and still, but the harlot will move 'in order not to conceive . . . and at the same time to render Venus more attractive to men'. Uncontrolled female sexuality is seen as bad because it threatens the foundations of patriarchy in the laws of inheritance and the institutionalization of male dominance (male ownership of women is even now enshrined in many of our laws and judicial attitudes), and so women have been consistently presented, in word and image, as innately passive. Freudian analysts have perpetuated this view (a view contradicted by recent anthropological and archeological studies which have yet to gain popular currency[4]). Helene Deutsch is typical: 'The theory that I have long supported – according to which femininity is largely associated with passivity and masochism – has been confirmed in the course of years of clinical observation.'[5] Passivity has indeed been imposed by lack of opportunity to be active, by strong social sanctions against certain activities; hysteria, so often observed by Freud in his female patients, was one of the prime symptoms of action denied. The greater freedoms and opportunities accorded to women this century have been largely superficial, leaving the essential power relations unchanged.

The polarization of active/male and passive/female is manifest in one of the earliest depictions of the mechanics of single-point perspective, Dürer's *Draughtsman drawing a nude*; the male artist is presented as active, analytical, the female model as passive, the object of his gaze and material for his creative intelligence. He sits upright, actively looks at her, while she reclines with eyes closed. Female passivity in contrast to male activity is similarly constructed in a passage from Benjamin West's discourse to the Royal Academy students in 1794: 'Were the young artist, in like manner, to propose to himself a subject in which he would represent the peculiar excellencies of women, would he not say, that these excellencies consist in a virtuous mind, a modest mien, a tranquil deportment, and a gracefulness in motion? And in embodying the combined beauty of these qualities, would he not bestow on the figure a general, smooth and round fulness of form, to indicate the softness of character; bend the head gently forward in the common attitude of modesty; and awaken our ideas of the slow and graceful movements peculiar to the sex, by limbs free from that masculine and sinewy expression which is the consequence of active exercise? – and such is the Venus de Medici.'

The *Medici Venus* is a particularly telling exemplar of female nudity for she represents a spurious modesty, her arms ineffectually attempting to conceal breasts and pudenda. Her gestures in fact serve to emphasize rather than to conceal her sex. In this she is typical. Most images of naked women by men are designed to display their bodies to the male gaze without challenge or confrontation. The female nude is an object of desire, a focus of male sexuality. As Laura Mulvey observed, in her seminal study 'Visual Pleasure and Narrative Cinema': 'In a world ordered by sexual imbalance, pleasure in looking is split between active/male and passive/female. The determining male gaze projects its fantasy onto the female figure, which is styled accordingly.'[6] As a genre the female nude (there is no male equivalent) has no purpose beyond the more or less erotic depiction of nakedness for male consumption. The male artist constructs for his own or for his male patron's enjoyment the perfect partner – passive, receptive, available. This explains the popularity of the Pygmalion myth in Victorian painting; the sculptor creates for himself a woman so perfect that he falls in love with her. Her naked perfection is his creation, literally passive until activated by his desire.

As John Berger has demonstrated, the essential difference between the male and female body, naked and clothed, is that 'men act and women appear'.[7] The nude female body is commonly presented as sexual spectacle, the picture set up as an invitation to voyeurism. The woman herself is often oblivious of the spectator, an innocent Susannah with the viewer in the role of lascivious Elder, enjoying the woman's nakedness and seeking to possess it. In representations of the Bathsheba and Susannah stories guilt and blame are displaced onto the passive female subjects; their nakedness is regarded as a culpable incitement to male lust. Men say of them, as of Eve, 'the woman tempted me'. In fact Christianity distorted the Old Testament story which emphasized David's adulterous desire and his consequent murder of Bathsheba's husband, shifting the blame to the woman by characterizing her as a seductress. Eve's role has been similarly distorted – she is popularly regarded as the cause of Adam's sin and her crime given sexual overtones: countless images of the Fall characterize Eve as temptress, her body provocatively displayed, her hair (a potent sexual symbol) in wild disarray. In the engraving by Floris she flirts openly, sitting on Adam's lap, her breast offered as an equivalent to the forbidden fruit. (Such attitudes still inform our rape laws, in which a woman's demeanour or dress can be interpreted as provocative or as 'contributory negligence', so that the reality is frequently that the *victim* appears to be guilty until proven innocent.) Such a displacement of blame is only possible where the naked woman's glance does not engage the viewer leaving him (such pictures presuppose a male audience; a woman must identify with the exhibitionism and narcissism, the vulnerability and victimization of the model) free to gaze at her body and to fantasize about it unchallenged.

Consequently a common device in representations of the nude female is to show her sleeping, as in Ingres's *Odalisque*, and Barry's *Reclining Nude*, and of course in one of the most admired nudes in history, Giorgione's *Venus*. Alternatively, she may avert her gaze or hide her eyes, or turn away from the viewer so that her face is not seen. Sometimes the head may be covered, or perhaps unfinished, even cut off by the edge of the picture – all these devices render their subject anonymous, denying individuality and status, and reducing the body to a stereotype. Occasionally she looks out at the spectator: in the Zuccarelli drawing her expression is coquettish and inviting, implying a receptivity to male desire. The Boucher *Venus* is posed in overt invitation to an unseen male viewer outside the picture frame. What all these images – the inviting or the unaware – have in common is that their bodies are displayed to the gaze of the viewer, the pose carefully contrived so as not to interfere with his visual access. Ingres's *Odalisque* is a case in point; her pose, which suggests voluptuous abandon, is actually rather uncomfortable, her arms thrown back and to her sides so as not to obscure her breasts, her body twisted onto one side to emphasize the curve of the hip. Likewise, Cecil Rea's model raises her arms and stretches, tautening the line of the breast seen in profile, and enhancing her waist. Display is the *raison d'être* behind such popular compositions as *The Three Graces* (effectively a device to show an all-round view of the female body), the *Judgement of Paris*, and hero/victim subjects such as *Perseus and Andromeda* or *Angelica and Ruggiero*, where the naked woman is chained to a rock in such a way that her nakedness is revealed most fetchingly. Venus and Cupid and The Judgement of Paris are subjects used almost exclusively for the display of female nudity in a valid and 'respectable' narrative context.

24

Thus the objections to Manet's famous nude *Olympia* were founded not in her class, her profession, or indeed her nakedness but in her unashamed awareness of the spectator's desire. Encountering her bold and challenging stare he cannot project the guilt that in a Christian culture is the inevitable concomitant of sexual desire, onto her. Olympia does not collude with the male viewer by lowering her gaze in the modest, submissive way expected of women, especially naked women (the 'modest mien' of West's discourse). Staring is a male prerogative, a strategy for dominating women, controlling and circumscribing their actions and thus it is Olympia's gaze which has been characterized by male critics as immodest. Only that bold look, and an alert rather than languorous pose, distinguishes her from thousands of admired nudes; she deflects the spectator's guilt from herself, like a mirror, by looking at the looker, and was thus castigated as 'impure', 'bestial', 'whore', 'an animal vestal'. The *Olympia* points up the stereotype embodied in most images of naked women in our culture, where female sexuality is set up as passive, exhibitionist, narcissistic. Passive nudity in the female is equated with availability. This is reflected in advertising images which associate the product with a naked or sexually-provocative woman; the implication is that both are desirable and available. For men they are synonymous as objects to be purchased; for women it is the image that is available, to be emulated.

Degas's nudes, especially the great series of pastels of women washing and drying themselves, have been characterized as a departure from the voyeuristic tradition of the female nude. They resist display, turn their backs, seem unaware of the possibility of observation, unlike the traditional nude who may close her eyes or turn her head but yet manages to display her body to advantage for the viewer to enjoy. Degas's women are not arbitrarily nude and their actions are wholly appropriate to the business of washing and drying their bodies. Degas's alleged misogyny is actually a refusal to comply with the unwritten rule that the female nude be reduced to a sexual spectacle, displaying the body to a male spectator. Degas himself subscribed to this view, describing them as 'a human creature preoccupied with herself – a cat who licks herself; hitherto the nude has always been represented in poses which presuppose an audience, but these women of mine are honest and simple folk, unconcerned by any other interests than those involved in their physical condition' but adds, fatally, 'It is as if you looked through a keyhole'.[8] Though he means merely to suggest that they act naturally, their poses not dictated or circumscribed by an awareness of male scrutiny, the import of this is rather different. While seeming to subvert the traditional nude he in fact presents us with a woman spied upon in a private act and the nakedness retains its voyeuristic frisson of forbidden pleasure.

(ii)   Compare these with the images of the male nude as constructed by the male artist. The pose is almost always active or dynamic: the model is shown fighting, labouring, gesturing or otherwise contorting his body to emphasize his musculature and to demonstrate the 'sinewy expression which is the consequence of active exercise', as West defined the character of the male nude. As the pattern of excellence and physical perfection the male body was symbolic of spiritual and cultural aspiration, most especially in the Renaissance, and was more usually the subject of anatomical studies. In images of the male nude the emphasis is on how the body works rather than how it appears. It is not devised for contemplation as a sexual object in the way that the female nude invariably is. The male nude was the staple of an academic training (indeed in the French Salon, the male nude study was known as an *academie*) the female life model not appearing until the later eighteenth century.

The male body, while not constructed as the site of sexual pleasure, is often symbolic of phallic power. The whole body, muscular, potent, active, may come to represent the phallus. Where softness, curves, smoothness are celebrated in a woman's body, strength and muscular development are the prerequisites of the male. Like its female counterpart, the male nude is evidence of the way patriarchy has imposed, and continues to reinforce through a proliferation of visual imagery, a series of opposites to define sexuality: masculine versus feminine, active versus passive, sexual drive versus sexual receptiveness.

The relative invisibility of the male nude in our culture is attributable to the fact that in a patriarchal society men have the power to define, and to define is to control. The 1988 exhibition 'Behold the Man: The Male Nude in Photography', at the Photographers' Gallery, London, and elsewhere, attempted to disprove this assertion of invisibility with an impressive array of material depicting the naked male body, but the majority of the examples were in fact produced for a specialized and limited audience and drawn from private rather than public collections – medical and anthropological studies, magazines for body-building enthusiasts, images from the gay sub-culture (both of the latter displays of men for men). It remains true that images of the male body are relatively rare in mainstream culture and those images that do appear are almost always celebrations of physical power – the vulnerability of nudity is screened out of representations of the male (to the extent that the erect penis – unable to match up visually to its role as symbol of phallic power – is forbidden even in so-called 'soft' pornographic publications). Images of the male nude are constructed to work against the stereotype of vulnerability, passivity and availability, over-emphasizing strength and physique in extremes of body-type or by means of accessories bearing phallic connotations. In advertising, the male body is used exclusively in situations where it connotes health, strength, invulnerability, whereas the naked female body is used indiscriminately, often unrelated to the product it promotes, simply to attract male attention and to suggest availability.

(iii)   However there is also a category of passive male nude, essentially the invention of Christianity, though occasional examples are to be found in classical art. The central image of the Christian religion is a tortured male nude, a feminized man who has passively, even masochistically accepted humiliation, punishment and death. But images of the passive male nude resist the obvious associations: the crucified Christ connotes self-sacrifice, physical fortitude and heroism, not vulnerability and weakness. Though his nakedness symbolizes his adopted humanity, his divinity is reaffirmed by the ultimate invulnerability of the body rising from the dead, marked but whole. Christian iconography glorifies the sufferings of the body (and en-courages a separation of mind and body, good and bad, divine and human) – the gruesome martyrdoms of the saints, the hair shirts and scourgings of the monastic life – frequently in the form of a naked body. In Christian art the only legitimate subjects for the inclusion of the naked human body were the Fall and the Expulsion, the Last Judgement, Purgatory, Hell and the Cruci-fixion, on account of the Christian doctrine that saw death and damnation as the inevitable result of an indulgence in the sins of the flesh. The body and its impulses were bad and must be subdued, mortified.

The passive male nude is born of this aspect of Christianity, and can be read as a type of Christ. His passivity is involuntary or imposed, rather than the seemingly innate passivity of the female. Since a languid passivity is not part of our vocabulary of masculinity we inevitably read such images in this way but though superficially analogous to the reclining female nudes they are in fact constructed differently. There is an emphasis on awkwardness, strain, discomfort, a vulnerability enhanced by the body's nakedness. We read these bodies not as sleeping, but as dead or injured: fallen warriors, sacrifices, martyred saints.

The tormented naked body expresses spiritual anguish by means of physical pain and contortion: see, for example, Michelangelo's *Rebellious Slave* and the *Laocoon*. Christianity used the nude as an ideograph of spiritual suffering, an image which turned society away from body-worshipping paganism. Because the gods of earlier pagan civilizations were depicted nude, the naked body gained a diabolical association in the eyes of the Church, and the story of the Fall, as recounted in Genesis, makes explicit a connection between awareness of the body's nakedness and a state of sin. The survival of the Platonic contention that spiritual things were degraded by taking corporeal shape was amalgamated, as so much else in Hellenic philosophy, with Christian morals. As a consequence the body's status was degraded from the mirror of divine perfection to a source of humiliation and shame. This state is most clearly expressed in the male nude, whose passivity or pain is expressive of pathos; only occasionally does an artist such as Rembrandt, or Van Gogh in *Sorrow* (Walsall Art Gallery), imbue the female flesh with this spirit.

(iv)   The active female nude does appear, of course, but in two particular and limiting guises. She is presented as the embodiment, the allegorical personification, of purely male qualities, or attributes and functions permitted only to men in the social order of the time: Revolution, Victory, Virtue, Justice. She acts not as a woman but in her capacity as the representative of a male quality. It was explained by Cesare Ripa in his *Iconologia* as follows: 'as every virtue is an appearance of the true, the beautiful and the desirable, in which the intellect takes its delight, and as we commonly attribute beauty to the ladies, we can conveniently represent one by the other'.[9]

Otherwise, active female nudity indicates voracious sexuality embodied in such mythic archetypes as Eve, the Sphinx, Salome, the *femme fatale* of *fin de siècle* and Symbolist art, Munch's provocative but deadly Madonna, Klimt's rapacious prostitutes. These predatory nudes embody the dangerous 'otherness' of women's sexuality unleashed. They menace and engulf their male 'victim' with their unbridled, and by implication, 'unnatural' lusts.

For every image that confronts the stereotypical polarization of active male/passive female thousands more conform. A series of photographic nudes by Oscar Rejlander recently republished by the Royal Photographic Society is a good example: the females (six from a set of ten) are all languidly passive, eyes or heads veiled or averted in maidenly modesty, while the males are vigorously active or, if seated, directly confront the camera. Even the French Socialist party posters, published in 1988, maintain these familiar stereotypes within a radical advertising campaign. Representing Liberty, a naked male athlete races forward clutching a rose in his outstretched hand. His pose is both vigorous and dynamic. Fraternity is symbolized by a similarly-naked but heavily pregnant woman seen in profile. This does indeed break one taboo but in presenting woman as passive mother it is readily assimilable to the traditional view.

ALBRECHT DÜRER (1471–1528)
Draughtsman drawing a nude 1525
Woodcut
(The Trustees of the British Museum,
London)

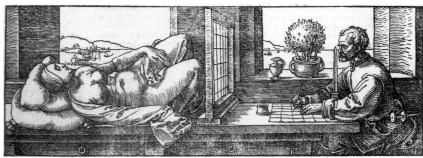

ALBRECHT DÜRER (1471–1528)
Apollo and Diana
Engraving

This image epitomizes the
active/passive opposition: the vigorous
hunter Apollo dominates the
composition, Diana simply sits in the
background. Here we are also offered
the association of woman with nature,
for Diana holds a bunch of grass to feed
the stag she is petting.

ANONYMOUS: FRENCH 1498
Hercules at the crossroads, from
Sebastian Brant, *Stultifer Navis*
(Rijksmuseum-stichting, Amsterdam)

Vice (or Lust) is commonly represented
as a masked woman, not in the abstract
sense that she might be used to personify
Victory or Truth, but as a natural

corollary to the belief that female
sexuality was both irresistible and
deadly. In *The choice of Hercules between
Vice and Virtue*, a subject where sexual
pleasure is seen as the path to death,
Vice is a naked or semi-draped woman,
her nakedness both the means by which
she tempts men to sin (and death) and
the outward sign of her sinfulness.

HENRI FUSELI (1741–1825)
Sin pursued by Death
Stipple-engraving and aquatint

The medieval theologians established
woman, naked and voluptuous, as the
personification of sin, and Death's
weapon against men, tempting them to
damnation.

FRANS FLORIS (c.1517–70)
Adam and Eve
Engraving

AFTER RAPHAEL (1483–1520)
Adam and Eve
Engraving

WILLIAM BLAKE (1757–1827)
The Temptation of Eve
Tempera on copper

In the events which precipitate the Fall, Eve is active, Adam passive. Floris's flirtatious Eve offers her breast to Adam's mouth, as the equivalent of the apple; the fruit of knowledge unleashed sin and death through the medium of woman's unbridled lust. In the Raphael, as in many interpretations of the Temptation and the Fall, the serpent has a woman's head and breasts; evil is thus unmistakably identified with the female principle, and, specifically, active female sexuality. The contrast between the active wicked woman and the passive innocent man is most pointed in Blake. Adam lies prone behind a seductive Eve standing within the phallic coils of the serpent. Clearly the result of autonomous female sexuality is death for man (prefigured here in Adam's sleep). Blake's Eve, with the all-encompassing serpent, looks back to the Pelasgian myth of the goddess of all things, Euronyme, coupling with the great serpent Ophion, a precursor of the Hebrew creation myth.

JACOPO TINTORETTO (1518–94)
Susannah and the Elders 1555–6
Oil on canvas
(Kunsthistorisches Museum, Vienna)

Icons of chastity – Susannah, Lucretia – became the pretext for a titillating display of naked female flesh. The impact of these moral fables was lost behind a misogynistic emphasis on the woman's guilt as embodied in her provocative nakedness. In this and in other versions of the Susannah subject, the woman makes ineffectual attempts to cover her body, her concealing/revealing gestures recalling the *Venus de Medici*.

Tintoretto's Susannah is oblivious to her predatory audience; as spectators, we collude in the voyeurism of the Elders. The woman is clearly blamed for her predicament and presented as an exhibitionist: vain, worldly, narcissistic. Elaborately coiffed, adorned with jewelled bracelets, she is rapt in contemplation of her image in the mirror. If she finds her own beauty so spellbinding, how can the Elders be blamed for succumbing to its temptations?

PETER PAUL RUBENS (1577–1640)
Bathsheba
Oil on wood
(Gemäldegalerie, Dresden)

Bathsheba's public (though
unintentional) display of her naked
body compromises her virtue and
tempts a man, King David, to sin,
first in his seduction of her, and
second in his collusion in the death
of her husband. Rubens's Bathsheba
sits with her legs and breasts bare,
adorned in furs and pearls, her smile
vaguely coquettish and collusive in
her imminent adultery.

F. FOSTER AFTER RAPHAEL
(1483–1520)
The Three Graces
Engraving

FRANÇOIS LEMOYNE (1688–1737) ▷
Perseus and Andromeda
Oil on canvas
(The Trustees, The Wallace
Collection, London)

A. LOMMELIN (*c.*1637–?)
AFTER PETER PAUL RUBENS
(1577–1640)
The Judgement of Paris
Engraving

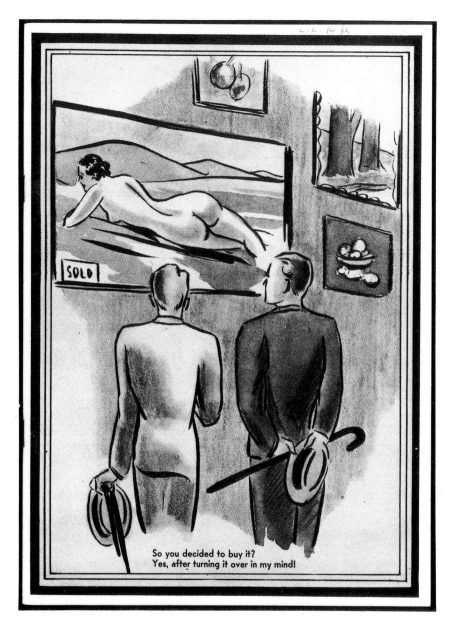

ANONYMOUS
Cover to catalogue of Allen Jones
exhibition at Waddington Galleries

What this image and the preceding
three have in common is an
assumption that the female nude has
a single function – titillating display.
See also the picture opposite.

SIR JOHN TENNIEL (1820–1914)
Pygmalion and the Statue 1878
Watercolour

In the original myth of Pygmalion and the statue, it is Aphrodite who animates the figure. In the course of time, Pygmalion became a symbol of the romantic lover who could create his ideal beauty through the intensity of his desire. Here, perfect female beauty is offered as man's creation, a statue as the ultimate passive, obedient woman, modelled to conform to male desires. Overtones of possession and control as the ideal position for men *vis-à-vis* women's sexuality are made explicit in Lawrence Gowing's remark on Matisse as a sculptor:

'Sculpture placed at the painter's disposal embodiments of sensual life which were more completely his own than the most submissive models.' (Lawrence Gowing, *Matisse* (London, 1979) p.79)

JEAN-AUGUSTE-DOMINIQUE INGRES
(1780–1867)
A Sleeping Odalisque
Oil on canvas

GIORGIONE (*c.*1476/8–1510)
Sleeping Venus
Oil on canvas
(Gemäldegalerie, Dresden)

HENRI MATISSE (1869–1954)
La Nuit 1922
Transfer lithograph

MANUEL ALVAREZ BRAVO (b.1902)
Good Reputation Sleeping (La Buena
Fama Durmiendo) 1938
Gelatin silver print

The sleeping female nude has been a
popular motif since the sixteenth
century. The familiar pose was designed
to flatter voyeuristic instincts and
suggests the sensual abandon of sexual
fulfilment, unselfconsciously
exhibitionist, shameless. Alternatively
it hints at the unselfconscious innocence
of unawakened desire.

ATTRIBUTED TO GUSTAV KLIMT
(1862–1918)
Two reclining female nudes
Blue chalk

'To his fragrance, she surrenders'   ▷
Advertisement for Bel Ami; an eau de
toilette for men (from *Cosmopolitan*
1987)

Klimt's nudes are displayed, erotic and inviting, in sensual abandon, with legs splayed. Sensuality and an acquiescent receptivity are represented as female virtues. Here, underscored by the advertising copy, the woman is a passive and vulnerable victim of male power and sexual domination. The image becomes a celebration of rape.

Many magazine editors found it offensive but were overruled by their publishers when Hermès threatened to withdraw all its advertising from every title in the stable to which the offended editor belonged. Many readers referred the advertisement to the Advertising Standards Authority but no action was taken. The company is, however, believed to be reconsidering the use of this advertisement for the American launch.

Bel Ami.
To His Fragrance. She Surrenders.

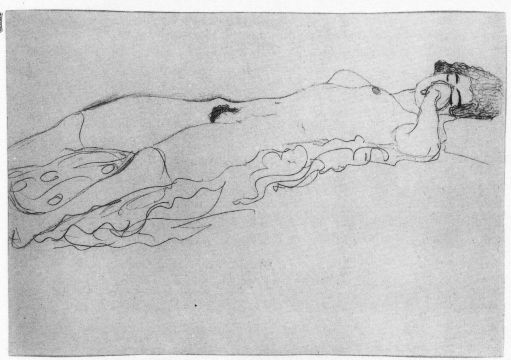

Gustav Klimt. Nu couché avec main gauche sur le visage. 1912-1913

Bel Ami.
An Eau De Toilette For Men.

WILLIAM MULREADY (1786–1863)
Seated female nude
Chalks

ERIC GILL (1882–1940)
Reclining female nude 1927
Pencil and red chalk

Here, as in the Mulready and the Léger, the woman's body is open to the male gaze but the covering or blanking out of her face serves both to render her anonymous and to complete the fiction that she is oblivious to the spectator.

FERNAND LÉGER (1881–1955)
Proto-Cubist study of a seated female nude 1908
Pen and ink

44

? WATSON
Nude Study *c.*1856–8
Albumen print

The photographer adopts a convention from painting, having his model admire herself in a mirror. We find this as a recurring device in paintings of the female nude, transforming the subject into a 'vanitas'; the male painter/viewer/patron enjoys the spectacle of the woman's nakedness, but condemns her vanity (constructed as a specifically female vice) as demonstrated by her admiration of her own beauty. We find the device used in conjunction with such famous nudes as Tintoretto's Susannah (see p.34), Titian's *Venus with a mirror* (National Gallery of Art, Washington) and the Velazquez *Rokeby Venus* (The National Gallery, London). The mirror acts as a 'vanitas' emblem, and compels the woman to 'connive in treating herself as first and foremost, a sight' (Berger).

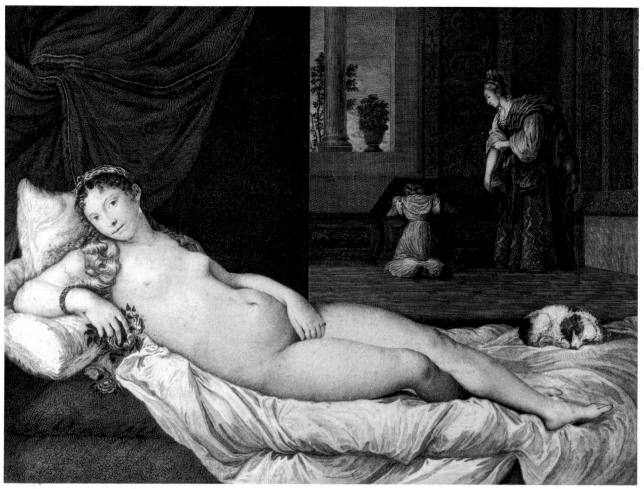

ANONYMOUS, AFTER TITIAN (1518–94)
The Venus of Urbino
Engraving

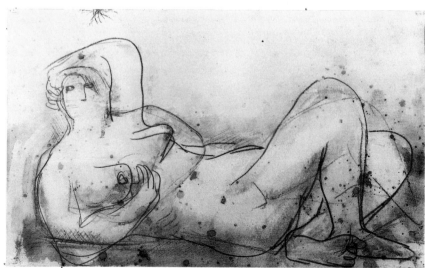

HENRY MOORE (1898–1986)
Reclining nude *c.*1930
Pencil and wash

E.J. BELLOCQ (1873–1940)
Nude girl reclining, dressed in mask and
stockings *c*.1911–13
Printing-out paper, gold toned, printed
from original negative by Lee
Friedlander

FRANCESCO ZUCCARELLI (1702–88)
Seated female nude
Chalks

In all of these pictures (pp.46–7) the
woman looks out at the viewer, or at an
unseen male protagonist. Zuccarelli is
aware of her naked charms; her
expression, though direct, is inviting
and very faintly provocative.

Bellocq made a series of portraits in
the brothels of Storyville, New Orleans;
the girls offer themselves frankly to the
camera's neutral gaze, flirtatious or
bored, inviting or passive. The masked
girl with her professional smile of
welcome is rendered anonymous to
her purchaser. This combination of
passive display/invitation is typical of
pornographic photography today, the
alternative being a seemingly
self-absorbed sensuality.

EDGAR DEGAS (1834–1917)
Après le bain, femme s'essuyant
Charcoal

Degas, in his great series of bathers, subverted contemporary ideology surrounding the female nude. His nudes are not devised for a male spectator, real or imagined (though of course there *is* one), hence the contorted poses and unflattering angles which resist an erotic reading. Instead he is presenting the woman's own experience of her body; she is absorbed in physical sensations of rubbing, drying, crouching, twisting, combing her hair. These women have a connection with their bodies that is lacking in the traditional female nude who exists only in relation to the omniscient male desire for which she is displayed. Critics resented the autonomy, the earthy physicality of these undesirable bodies, describing them as 'ugly', 'swollen' and 'debased'.
See also p.53.

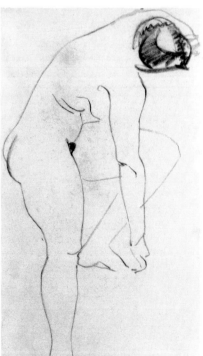

HENRI GAUDIER-BRZESKA (1891–1915)
Life study; female figure
Charcoal

Gaudier-Brzeska's unromanticized model shares with Degas's bathers a self-absorbed awareness of her own stretched and drooping flesh. Physical sensation rather than appearance is the artist's subject here.

BARBARA HEPWORTH (1903–75) ▷
Figure study of two nude women 1949
Pencil on white grounded board

These figures have a balance and solidity rare in images of the female nude; there is nothing provocative about them.

Barbara Hepworth
Nov. 2. 1949

JOHN OPIE (1761–1807)
Life study of a standing male figure
Chalks

Compare this with the pictures on
pp.51–2, 55–7.

BACCIO BANDINELLI (1493–1560)
Studies (five on one sheet) of male
nude figures
Pen and ink

SIR EDWARD JOHN POYNTER
(1836–1919)
Male nude: Study for *The Catapult*
Chalk

SIR EDWARD JOHN POYNTER
(1836–1919)
Studies of a kneeling male nude
stretching
Chalk and pencil

EDGAR DEGAS (1834–1917)
The Tub c.1891
Pastel
(The Burrell Collection, Glasgow
Museums & Art Galleries)

KEN KIFF (b.1939)
Man Greeting Woman 1965–66
Oil, tempera, and gesso on board
(Collection: Arts Council of Great
Britain)

Kiff's man and woman re-enact the traditional stereotypical relationship: man active, woman passive, but he highlights her uncertainty – the man is single-minded, purposeful, aggressive; she, though her pose is open, inviting, as she has been taught, seems to have been disturbed from self-absorbed reverie, her natural state misinterpreted by the predatory male. She offers a lipsticked mouth, conventional signifier of desire/availability, but her expression is anxious and apprehensive. The innocence of the title is belied in the actual; we are alerted to the undercurrents of sexual dominance and harassment lurking in all social interaction between men and women.

ANONYMOUS: ITALIAN SCHOOL
(LOMBARDIC) late 16C
Crouching male nude with hammer and
chisel
Red chalk

ROBERT MEDLEY (b.1905)
Study of male nude in a squatting
position seen from the back 1957
Charcoal

FREDERIC, LORD LEIGHTON (1830–96)
Studies (four on one sheet) of a male
nude with a sling
Chalks

ANONYMOUS: NATIONAL AERONAUTICS
AND SPACE ADMINISTRATION (NASA)
1972
Replica of engraved placard sent into
space with the Pioneer I spacecraft

This 'cosmic greeting card' was
designed to inform alien life-forms about
our galaxy and human beings. Even
here, at the point of the most advanced
technology, the established stereotype is

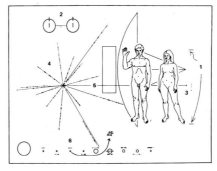

maintained; it is the man who takes the
superior and active role, raising his hand
in greeting, while his female companion
stands passive and docile by his side.

EADWEARD MUYBRIDGE (1830–1904)
Plate 522 from *Animal Locomotion* 1887
Photogravure

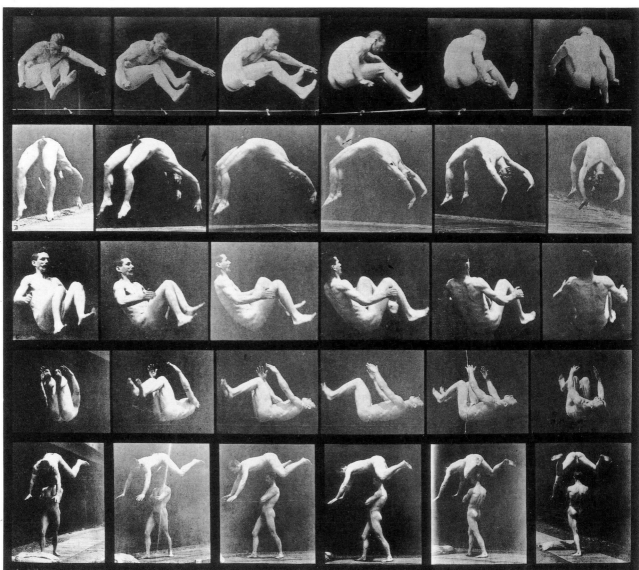

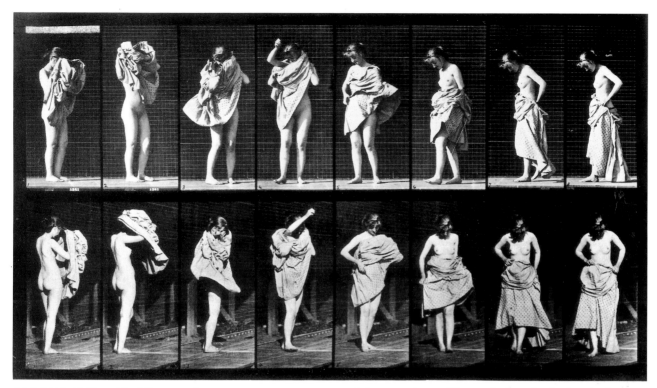

EADWEARD MUYBRIDGE (1830–1904)
Plate 425 from *Animal Locomotion* 1887
Photogravure

EADWEARD MUYBRIDGE (1830–1904)
Plate 529 from *Animal Locomotion* 1887
Photogravure

▽

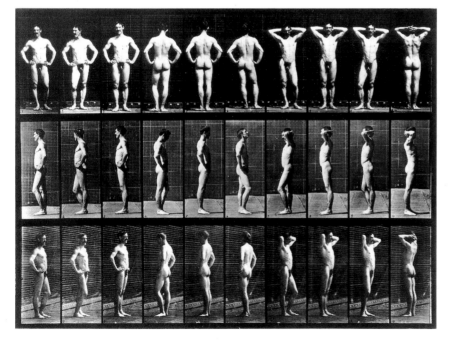

The gendering of active/passive is even to be found in an ostensibly dispassionate scientific exercise such as Muybridge's great *Animal Locomotion* series. Men are shown in strenuous athletic or labouring activities, women in the more sedate tasks of domesticity. The alliance of photography and scientific enquiry remained very firmly within the traditional male/female stereotypes as perpetuated by painting; the only concessions are the rare images of the male body in repose or displayed for the camera, but here notions of passivity are effectively subverted by the evident muscularity of the male body, its potential for action. In Plate 529 the subject's gaze is confrontational, he looks directly at the camera, impassive, without recourse to the evasions of the female nude. His body is still, but not passive – it is flexed, tense, taut, to be studied rather than enjoyed.

59

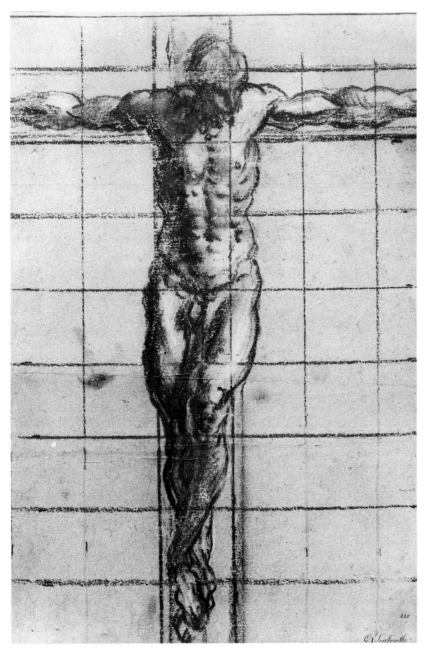

JACOPO TINTORETTO (1518–94)
Christ on the Cross
Black chalk, squared

JEAN HUGHES TARAVAL (1729–85)
Male life study
Chalk

CARLE VAN LOO (1705–64)
Study of two male figures from *Six Figures Academiques*
Etching

NICOLAES MAES (1634–93)
Study for the figure of Isaac in a
Sacrifice of Isaac
Pen and ink and wash, touched with red
chalk

Here, and in the preceding three pictures, the passive male nude is frequently presented in the guise of Christ or of a martyred saint, as if passivity in the male must be allied to courage, sacrifice, a cause transcending the individual. For men, 'victim' status is seen as something that is chosen, rather than being 'innate' as it appears to be in women.

Compare this with the pictures on pp.64–7.

63

CHARLES RICKETTS (1866–1931)
Nude male reclining
Pencil

BENEDETTO LUTI (1666–1724)
Male nude huddled on ground
Red chalk

THOMAS STOTHARD (1755–1834)
Nude male reclining
Pen and ink

FILIPPO AGRICOLA (1776–1857)
Study of the Laocoon group
Red chalk

PALMA GIOVANE (1548–1628)
Study for the figure of the rebellious
slave carved by Michelangelo for the
tomb of Julius II
Pen, ink and wash

ANONYMOUS, AFTER NICOLAS POUSSIN
(1594–1665)
Venus arming Aeneas
Engraving

DOSSO DOSSI (*c.*1479–*c.*1542)
Circe and her lovers in a landscape
(detail)
Oil on canvas
(National Gallery of Art, Washington,
Samuel H. Kress Collection)

Circe was a beautiful sorceress whose magic powers were used to turn men into swine (this fate befalls Odysseus' companions when they land on her island; Odysseus himself resists and defeats her blandishments with the help of the gods). She was a type of *femme fatale,* irresistible but deadly, another example of woman's fair nakedness as the route to death and damnation. (The pig is sacred to the death goddess, Hecate, and thus an identification of Circe with Hecate is suggested.) The Circe story became symbolic of debasing love, a warning that to succumb to the charms of a beautiful woman reduces a man to an animal state, distracting him from higher spiritual ambitions, and transforms him from a creator of culture into a product of nature.

EDVARD MUNCH (1863–1944)
Madonna 1895
Lithograph

Munch's women are icons of vivacious
and deadly sexuality. The Madonna,
predator rather than protector, looms
over her victim, flaunting her body
which is silhouetted against the dark
coils of her hair. Congress with her
will be fatal: death is inscribed in the
cavernous contours of her face and the
skull-like features of the cringing foetus.
She is the source of life but the foetus
suggests man's existence as a kind of
death-in-life. Woman is seen as the
agent of death, an irresistible but deadly
creature on whom male sexuality is
dependent – see the sperms dancing
attendance.

ROBERT MAPPLETHORPE (b.1946)
Lisa Lyon
Gelatin silver print
(Courtesy of the Robert Miller Gallery,
New York)

THE FETISHIZED FEMALE

Though the male nude can be eroticized – witness certain images of St Sebastian swooning in a state between pain and ecstasy as the arrows pierce his flesh, or Robert Mapplethorpe's male nudes informed by a homosexual sensibility – only the female is fetishized, mutilated, fragmented, rendered anonymous. The objectification and fragmentation of women's bodies is perhaps an inevitable corollary of women's status in Western society and thus in Western art; as in the Dürer, the woman is the passive object, man the analytical creator (in the gendering of the artist/model opposition), projecting his vision, his tastes, his desires, his view of the world, onto her body. Hence the woman's body is not accorded the respect for its wholeness that the male nude receives.

This fragmentation of the female body ranges from the formal exercises which constitute a large part of Bill Brandt's work with the nude to images which celebrate mutilation or disabling. Brandt works with form and texture, focusing on parts of the body which lose their identity in the process and become mysterious unidentifiable configurations. The sexual identity of these forms is obscured by analogies to the abstract beauty of organic growths – shells, stones, fungi. At the same time Brandt was producing studies of the female nude which offer fragmentation or anonymity as a threat. In these photographs the head is hidden by hair or by a featureless black mask, creating an air of violence and compulsion. Most striking is an example from 1977 in which the torso fills the frame, cut off at the neck and at mid-thigh, and the arms are masked in black cloth to appear amputated. Here the inspiration must have been the fragmentary classical sculptures, among them the *Venus de Milo*, but the implied mutilation of living flesh has a power to disturb above that of a damaged statue. It is perhaps no coincidence that the *Venus de Milo* has become an archetype of female beauty, possessing an iconic familiarity and reproduced in countless contexts from high art to advertising. Given pride of place in the Greek court of the Crystal Palace, she was described in the catalogue as affording 'perhaps the most perfect combination of grandeur and beauty in the female form' but is there not some significance in the fact that this icon of female beauty is armless, in other words mutilated and thus literally powerless and passive. Images of women's bodies, cropped and truncated, are so familiar we scarcely remark upon them, but it is rare to encounter similar images of men; though individual limbs may be studied, it is unusual to find the male body denied a sense of wholeness, of identity.

In Robert Mapplethorpe's work the male nude becomes erotic spectacle, passive, posed, yet phallic power is celebrated in physique and the implicit potential for action. But he is capable of applying the same principles to the female body; in the series of photographs of the body-builder Lisa Lyon the eroticism is located not in her nakedness but in her body's strength, power and texture. In Mapplethorpe both male and female bodies are subject to fragmentation, treated as aesthetic objects; see, for instance, *Chest* (1987) in which three blown-up sections of a man's torso are considered in isolation as abstractions.

The fetishized nude is an extreme example of the female body distorted for male fantasy and gratification (both of which depend to some degree on control). Of course all studies of the nude reflect to some extent the sexual preferences of their makers and thus of their time, with an exaggerated emphasis on breasts or buttocks or stomach, slenderness or heavy flesh (Cranach for example, contrasted with Rubens and Courbet) but a creation such as Allen Jones's *Desire Me* is an extreme distortion of the female anatomy to satisfy male sexual appetites. The woman in *Desire Me* is constrained literally by her clothes and shoes but also conceptually by male desire and expectation. He projects his sexuality onto her image, fetishizing her sexual characteristics, hence the tight rubber leggings, the high heels, the unnatural (silicone-implanted?) breasts. This is a manufactured artificial femininity bearing no relation to the bodies of real women and thus imposing upon them a false and impossible ideal. Such super-femaleness (celebrated in advertising and pornography) subjugates women by creating in them feelings of inadequacy. Alternatively, a woman may reject this image and its message, denying the feminine in herself, and seek uneasily to create an alternative expression of femaleness that avoids the parody and caricature, the violence, of Jones's vision.

Tom Wesselmann's series of 'Great American Nudes' bear a superficial similarity to Allen Jones's provocative women but it can be argued that they offer a more intelligent analysis of the role of the female nude in art and culture than at first appears. His pictures have been acclaimed by (male) critics as the advance guard of permissiveness: his first life-size nudes, with erect nipples and exposed pubic hair, were painted in 1961 when the publishing of full-frontal nude photographs was still illegal. Though the female nude has dominated his work (and remains a favourite subject for his latest painted steel constructions), becoming an obsessive theme, he maintains that 'It is always the form that counts. The subject matter is of virtually no consequence' and suggests that his pictures would have the same meaning even if their subject matter were automobiles. This is an extraordinary claim in the face of the emotive and politically-loaded significance of the female nude; thus does Wesselmann both demonstrate and collude with the process whereby women's bodies are reduced to commodities in a consumer culture, objects to be bought and sold.

With their unabashed erotic content these pictures offer the stereotypical ideal of a passive anonymous female sexuality. Nevertheless, there is a certain ambiguity in these paintings, with their crude puns and blatant stereotypes; by such unsubtle devices Wesselmann seeks to make obvious the way in which the female body and female sexuality have been perverted, used and abused by a consumer society which reduces everything to object and appetite.

The disabling or distorting of the female nude in certain images indicates a fear of women's autonomous uncontrolled sexuality. Church and state, bastions of the patriarchal system, have always endeavoured to control woman's sexuality and thus her reproductive activity, by moral, legal and economic means. Unrestricted female sexuality has been seen by men as a dangerous force threatening the bases of their power, and women have as a result been categorized as the 'Other' (Freud, de Beauvoir) to be 'castrated' and rendered powerless. Since nudity is the prime signifier of sexuality such fears will obviously surface in images of the nude.

The female nude is highly visible in our culture, a much used and abused image. Her very familiarity as part of a long tradition made her the most obvious motif on which to experiment with pictorial languages. The mould-breaking modernist artists – Picasso, Matisse, the German Expressionists, the Surrealist Hans Bellmer with his dismembered *Dolls*, de Kooning in his 'Women' series, André Kertesz in the *Distortions*, and Dubuffet in his *Corps de Dames* – all worked with the female nude. As de Kooning observed, it suited his purposes better than an arbitrarily-invented shape: 'I thought I might as well stick to the idea that it's got two eyes, a mouth and a neck'.[10] (Note his casual denigration of the female body as an object, as 'it'.)

The theme of anonymity runs through the tradition of the female nude to the extent that a nude portrait arrests, even affronts. Again and again the male artist reduces the female model to an object, to 'it'. As Picasso put it: 'I try to do a nude as it is. If I do a nude, people ought to think: It's a nude not Madame Whatsit.' Images of the female nude, his exclusive obsessive subject matter in the late work, are woman reduced to sexual cipher, her body subjected to violence and distortion (though, in a review of the show *Late Picasso* at the Tate Gallery, London, 1988, David Sylvester was able to say of *Reclining Nude on a Blue Divan*, 1960, that 'as we look at her flesh and imagine involuntarily what it would be like to touch, we sense it to be deliciously soft and yielding', a clear demonstration of men's ability to appropriate *all* images of the female nude to an erotic appreciation) but whatever the violence done to her image, breasts, belly and sex are always identifiable, marking out her use and status.

At this point it is perhaps worth examining in more detail the confusion of ideologies surrounding images of the female nude, especially those which allegedly objectify women. In current feminist criticism all nudes are seen as objectifying women, whereas pictures of women at work or in a neutral social context are not. In truth, of course, all images objectify; they make an object – a drawing, a painting, a photograph – of reality. The real criticism to be levelled at the nude is that it presents a male fantasy of woman's sexuality, it objectifies the female body by rendering it anonymous and fragmentary. The gendered polarity of male artist/female model is only now being eroded, with women beginning to work with the nude and to challenge the male-defined stereotypes. However, because the majority of the images of the female nude which we see around us are expressive of the male view it does not necessarily follow that images of the female body are bad *per se*. It must be remembered that meaning is drawn from context, audience and encoded attitudes. The danger lies not in the objectifying of the body, an inevitable process of artistic practice but in certain images which encourage the viewer to read the body as an anonymous available object, images which degrade, exploit or mutilate the human body.

ANONYMOUS: GREEK *c.*100 BC
Venus de Milo
Marble
(Musées Nationaux, Paris)

The female body in pictorial imagery
(and indeed in pornographic fantasy)
is routinely fragmented, denied
wholeness. (For example, a whole
subculture of fantasy exists around the
idea of sexual congress with a woman
who has lost one or both legs.) In this
image (and those on pp.76–8, 83), the
body has been reduced to a torso, often
headless, but a torso styled to be sexually
provocative.

In the Gill and the Clausen, the unseen
arms are raised to reveal and to tauten
the line of the breasts, backs arched to
define the waist. The Brodzky woman,
a headless torso with truncated limbs, is
sprawled passive and inviting, legs
spread, nipples erect. She is an object
inviting sexual use.

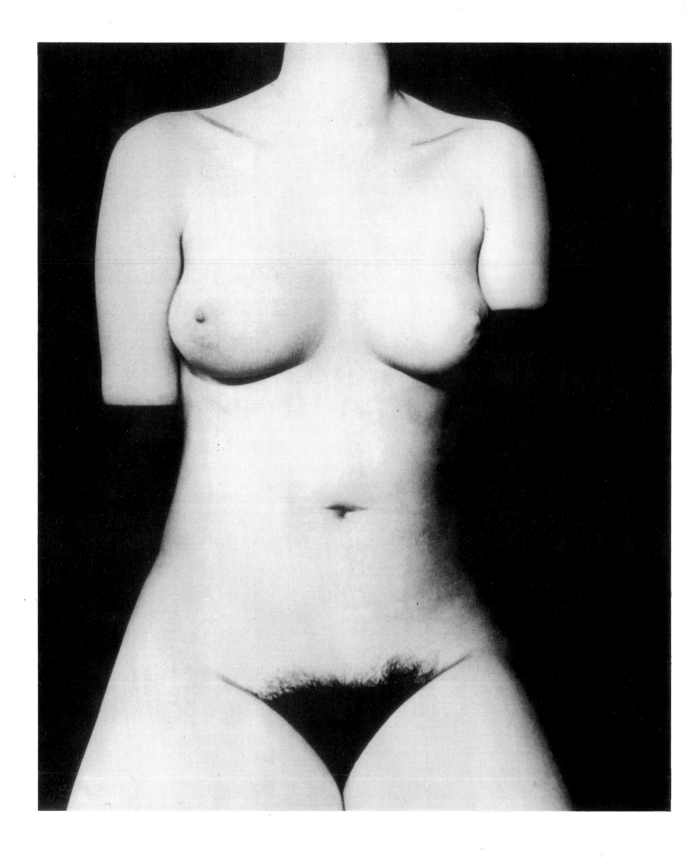

BILL BRANDT (1904–83)
Nude: London 1977
Gelatin silver print
(© Estate of Bill Brandt
By permission of Noya Brandt)

ANONYMOUS AFTER JACOPO PALMA
(1548–1628)
Studies of armless female nude statue
Pen and ink

THE FETISHIZED FEMALE

ERIC GILL (1882–1940)
Life study: torso of a woman 1927
Pencil

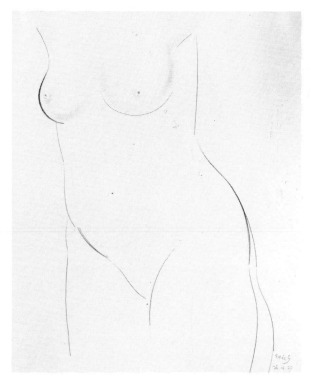

EDVARD MUNCH (1863–1944)
Madonna 1893/4
Oil on canvas
(By courtesy of the Munch-
Museet, Oslo).

HORACE BRODZKY (1885–1969)
Reclining nude 1917
Pencil

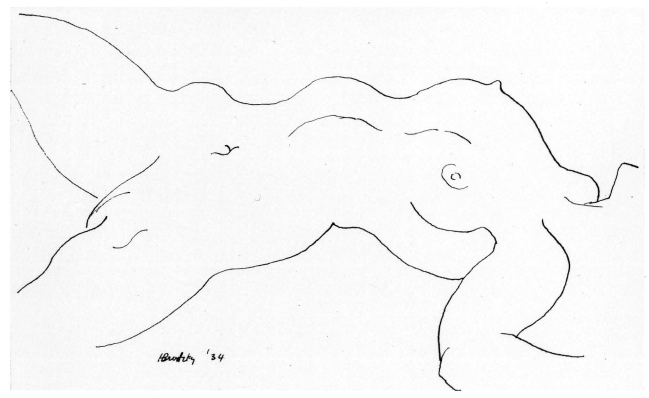

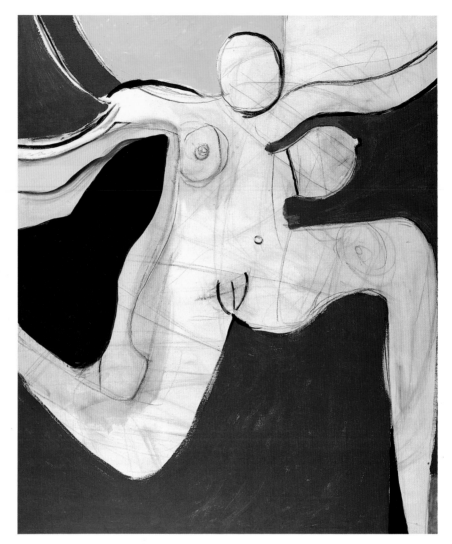

ROGER HILTON (1911–75)
Dancing Woman December 1963
Oil and charcoal on canvas
(Scottish National Gallery of Modern
Art, Edinburgh)

Here we see woman active, an exuberant
image which celebrates her sexuality
without being either a threat to the male
or an overt invitation.

TOM WESSELMANN (b.1931)
Pink Breast
Screenprint

Pink Breast is the two-dimensional equivalent of his 1970 installation *Bedroom Tit Box* in which a nude model is screened from view except for one breast suspended into a perspex box. Wesselmann's work expresses the way in which women are reduced to a series of sexual signifiers – mouth, breasts, pubic triangle – but it continues to celebrate this anonymous availability, rather than seeking to undercut it.

SIR EDWARD JOHN POYNTER
(1836–1916)
Water Babies 1900
Oil on canvas
(Photograph by courtesy of Frost &
Reed)

This is a perfect example of the coy
female nudity the Victorians favoured,
a nudity rendered innocently
unprovocative by the classical setting.
It also illustrates the nineteenth-century
obsession with the subject of the female
bather, found in academic and avant-
garde production, in both of which the
naked woman embodies the fecundity of
the natural world.

SIR GEORGE CLAUSEN (1852–1944)
Nude female torso
Pencil

HORACE BRODZKY (1885–1969)
Two boys 1933
Pen and ink
(Collection: Arts Council of Great
Britain)

Here Brodzky treats the male body with
a tenderness and respect lacking in his
study of the female nude (p.78). Like
their female counterpart, the two boys
are faceless, anonymous. There is no
emphasis on their sexuality – indeed
Brodzky has omitted their genitals
entirely. The effect is of sexuality
expressed in closeness and affection, in
contrast to the threatening 'otherness'
of the rapacious and demanding female
reduced to a sex object.

GLYN WARREN PHILPOT (1884–1937)
Male nude: back view
Pencil

The male nude as an object of
contemplation, the site of eroticism and
desire.

These images originate from a
homoerotic response to the male body,
although women may also respond
positively to them. Women's images of
men, on the other hand, tend to be either
deflating or uncomfortably
self-conscious.

84

E. J. BELLOCQ (1873–1940)
Nude study, New Orleans c.1911–13
Printed on paper, gold toned

This image, from the series of portraits
of whores in the bordellos of New
Orleans, was printed up from the
original broken negative by Lee
Friedlander in the 1960s (see also
p.47). It stands as a telling comment on
the aesthetic tastes of our own society
which privilege so distorted an image of
the female body on the same level as
images of the body intact and whole.

This anonymous torso is analogous to
the mutilated statues so admired by
earlier ages – headless, thighs split
from torso and themselves virtually
amputated by black stockings
(interesting that the stocking should be
one of the commonest of male sexual
fetishes!).

to canvas using the naked bodies of women, this piece by Self takes the objectification of the female body a stage further. This tripartite image was one of a suite of eleven etchings, the prelude to a proposed collection of '1000 Temporary Objects of Our Time'. In a statement for the São Paulo Bienale, 1971, Self described his interest in reproducing 'objects' and the idea of a kind of census of images of 'objects'. The body is fragmented and anonymous, seemingly trapped within the plate, rebelling against the artist. Overtones of compulsion and violence emerge in the shadows her body has left on the paper.

PEDRO PRUNA (b.1904)
Standing female nude, with arms bound behind her 1936
Indian ink and wash

This is one of several sketches recording the atrocities of the Spanish Civil War. The girl's nakedness is part of a process of shaming and humiliation and may very probably be a prelude to rape or other assault. Without the context, and other signs such as the shaved head, she is iconographically indistinguishable from other images in this section. Compare the tied and masked nude by Brandt. Both images relate female nakedness directly to the status of a victim, or powerless object.

COLIN SELF (b.1941)
Figure No.7 (a, b, c)
Etching

This image was formed by placing the body on an etching plate and spraying over it. When the body was removed, a clean shadow was left on the plate which was then etched. Thus the shadow of the body becomes the inked part of the image.

Though related to Yves Klein's 'body art' pictures in which paint was applied

▷

BILL BRANDT (1904–83)
Nude: Campden Hill, London 1978
Gelatin silver print
(© Estate of Bill Brandt
By permission of Noya Brandt)

TOM WESSELMANN (b.1931)
Great American Nude 56 1964
Liquitex and collage on board
(© DACS 1988. Photo courtesy of
Mayor Rowan Gallery, London)

This is one of a series, the 'Great American Nudes', in which the naked woman is modelled as the direct equivalent of the *Playboy* centre spread, legs wide to show the pubic hair (in many variations on the theme, real hair is collaged onto the canvas). The pubic area and the breasts are invariably emphasized by bikini-shaped triangles of white flesh. The faces are always blank but for a mouth open in a smile of invitation and ecstasy. A crude sexual symbolism is announced by the jar of flowers, including anemones with their strongly-defined stamens (the sexual organs) and roses, and by the two oranges placed side by side in close proximity to the breasts. This is woman reduced to a sexual object, a site of oral gratification, a consumer commodity.

ALLEN JONES (b. 1937)
Desire Me 1968
Pencil on card (upper part); watercolour
airbrushed over a photograph
(lower part)

Here we have what purports to be an
image of voracious female sexuality
constructed as fetishized male fantasy.
The figure has all the attributes of the
classic male fantasy – all her sexual
characteristics are exaggerated. The
open mouth, commonly seen in
pornographic photographs, is a signifier
of desire in the passive female.

   Desire Me is not a command by
the woman. She is styled as a
stereotypically-desirable object but it is
the artist/spectator who asks of her
'desire me'. She is trapped within male
expectations, disabled by stiletto heels,
literally encased in an alien skin of
rubber latex, and without arms (yet
again!), powerless to resist male
potency. Her open mouth, far from
expressing desire seems to be silently
screaming, recoiling from the
impending violation her appearance
invites. One thinks of rapists claiming
provocation or incitement on the
grounds that their victim was dressed in
a manner considered 'sexy'. Women are
effectively trapped in a double bind of
expectation – to attract a mate they
must look attractive, but when does
'attractive' become 'provocative'? Is
Jones implying that women are solely to
blame for their own oppression? Is he,
like Munch, perhaps threatened by the
active sexuality of women, and thus
seeking to exorcize his fears by
constructing an image of woman on
which to project his guilt?

ANDRÉ KERTESZ (b.1894)
Distortion No.6 1933
Gelatin silver print

PABLO PICASSO (1881–1973)
Les Demoiselles d'Avignon 1907
Oil on canvas
(Collection, the Museum of Modern
Art, New York. Acquired through the
Lillie P. Bliss Bequest)

NATURE VERSUS CULTURE

We won't play Nature to your Culture
   Photo-piece by Barbara Kruger, 1983

One of the most pervasive stereotypes in our social philosophy is the woman/nature, man/culture dichotomy. In every known society women are identified as being closer to nature than to culture. Just as nature is the source of life – fertile, instinctual – so is woman; her biological processes – menstruation, child-bearing, breast-feeding – allotting her the more obvious role in the reproductive process. Culture, however, devalues nature, and thus the patriarchal condition has arisen of man controlling woman and woman's sexuality, a control which continues to the present with male domination of gynaecology and the punitive laws against prostitution which criminalize the woman but not her client. In primitive societies man's role in procreation was not recognised and some anthropologists (e.g. Margaret Mead) have argued that civilization and culture were compensatory devices. With woman creating naturally and apparently independently through childbirth, men needed to devise for themselves an alternative function and purpose in the world. By the time of Plato, having established culture as his creation, man could proceed to claim the major role in reproduction with woman as 'merely the passive incubator of his seed'.

The identification of woman with nature (itself a vague abstraction signifying that part of the world which is irrational, not made, controlled or fully understood by man) has its roots in myth where nature is identified with the female body in the person of the Greek earth goddess Gaia. She is paired with the sky god Uranos – Mother Earth and Father Sky (note that myth assigns to the male deity the superior position) and thus where man is equated with spirit, woman is identified with matter. The female body (the earth) was, after Plato, long seen as the passive host to the male semen (the seed), giving generative powers to men and reducing woman to the status of a container, an incubator. This is reflected in the biblical characterization of woman as 'the weaker vessel', and the Virgin Mary as a vessel, inviolate, her womb activated by the supernatural power of a male god. As a castrated goddess Mary supplanted the vigorous and autonomous mother goddesses of earlier cultures; the rise of patriarchal institutions was accompanied by a decline in the mythic powers of these mother goddesses and a transfer of their functions of creation and fertility to the male consort or son, just as a naked male body (Christ) replaced the naked females of earlier civilizations as the central cult object. Indeed it was Christianity which propagated the dichotomization and gendering of mind and body, uniting elements of Greek philosophy and Jewish theology. Thus the medieval theologians, having defined woman as body could impute to her all the sins of the flesh, attributing original sin to Eve and sexual guilt to her female descendents because of their innate inability to resist their bodily impulses. Indeed Eve's punishment is specifically related to her sexuality, for God decrees that childbirth will be the source of pain and suffering for the woman: 'in sorrow thou shalt bring forth children' (Genesis 3:16). Woman's sexuality, when uncontrolled, threatened the bases of patriarchy, thus set her outside civilization, outside culture. She can only be seen as an agent of culture, and her sexuality a civilizing force, when it is used in the service of patriarchal power, as in the Assyrian *Epic of Gilgamesh* when the wild man Enkidu is seduced and thereby brought within the confines of society by the *harimtu* (temple prostitute).

One school of feminist thought has accepted this division of mind and body, suggesting that women, by their biological nature, are more closely allied with the instinctual, peaceable, nurturing habits characterized in our society as good. Groups such as the Greenham Common anti-nuclear campaigners, and indeed women generally, are held to be non-interventionist in their approach to the natural world, and thus passive in a good sense, co-operative. The converse of such a theory is of course to attribute to men the sins of aggression, castigating them as actual or potential rapists of women and the landscape. This ignores the fact that attitudes and behaviour, including gender roles, are, to some extent, culturally learned. Society has ascribed the nurturing role to women to reconcile them to motherhood and its restrictions, and to compensate them for their lack of economic and political power; this is evident in the nineteenth century when moral superiority was attributed to women in order to corral them in the domestic sphere. Men and women collude in this construction of society; witness the proliferation of women's art and literature in which women actively claim the passive role. But that woman is not predisposed to the maternal role by gender alone is demonstrated in such works as Mary Kelly's *Post-Partum Document* which examined the artist's experience of mothering and revealed it as a learned process, not an instinctual response. In the words of Adrienne Rich, 'Patriarchy could not survive without motherhood and heterosexuality in their institutional forms; therefore they have to be treated as axioms, as nature itself, not open to question.'[11]

However, the naked woman in the landscape has been a potent and popular image, reinforcing the equivalence of woman with nature. In Gravelot and Cochin's *Almanach Iconologique* (1768) Nature is personified as a naked woman with abundant hair, a symbol of fertility and sexuality. Like Eve before the Fall, she is at one with the plants and animals which surround her. The naked woman in the landscape came to be seen as appropriate, 'natural', the curves of her body echoing the natural configuration of the land. Giorgione's *Sleeping Venus* is the precursor of many such images – the bathers of Courbet, Renoir and Cézanne, the monumental nymphs of Matisse, Gauguin's Tahitian girls.

There is often a mythological *raison d'être* for the depiction of the nude in a landscape setting; the naked female is presented as Venus, Diana, or a nymph, figures who embody ideas of fertility or acquiescent sexuality, instinct or inspiration (*see* Reynolds's remarks on nature as the source of an artist's inspiration). The nereids and dryads of Greek myth, spirits of place and of natural phenomena, offer an allegorical purpose for the nude female in the landscape. Etty's nudes are of this kind, life-studies dressed up to mythic significance, but despite such accessories they excited the disgust of critics, with their sturdy contemporary bodies so different from the slender androgynous forms which, to the Victorian mind, denoted the innocent respectability of a distant classical past. In *The Deluge* Etty seems to suggest woman as an agent not only of the Fall but also of the Flood, while Legros's *La Source* offers a double allegory – woman as the personification of a spring and thus life-giving and fertile, elemental rather than a product of culture. By the time of Renoir, Cézanne, Millet, these naked women in natural outdoor settings are no longer 'explained' as goddesses or nymphs but still partake of the myth. They represent a return to woman before the Fall: pure, unselfconscious, a creature of animal instincts. The naked woman is thus presented as part of the natural order (itself a social construct, constituted of distinct and separate spheres of masculinity and femininity). The appearance of such pictures coincided with the rising tide of feminism and female emancipation; they are the response of the potent male, showing woman in her 'proper' sphere as a sensual, instinctual animal whose purpose was to stimulate the artist's libido (his creative urge) and to reproduce and nurture.

Photographers have made much use of the nude in the landscape, usually as a formal exercise and eschewing any conscious mythological associations. Brandt, for instance, is fascinated by analogies between the female body and other natural forms such as rocks and fossils; living flesh and senseless stone share the same textures, the same sense of solidity and monumentality. Edward Weston's nudes are objective studies undifferentiated from his photographs of driftwood or vegetables, though tainted by the nature of his subject, with voyeurism: from his high viewpoint the camera and the male intelligence behind it dominate the apparently oblivious model. Brassai's nudes, published in the short-lived periodical *Minotaure* share something of Brandt's concerns, offering the naked female body as a natural feature of the landscape, their curves echoing one another. But the pictorialist photographers such as Alfred Lys Baldry use the naked woman in the landscape in the same spirit of pseudo-mythology as his painter contemporaries. In their photo-diptychs *Industrialization* and *Subordination* (from *Remodelling Photo-History*, 1982) Jo Spence and Terry Dennett, using Jo's naked body, revealed the 'naturalness' of the nude in the landscape to be an artificial concept. They offer more realistic unromantic explanations for her presence, showing her unmistakably as victim, a body murdered, dumped, abandoned.

The nature/culture opposition is set out most clearly in pictures of naked women with clothed men in a landscape. Giorgione's *Concert Champêtre* and Manet's *Déjeuner sur l'Herbe* imply that the woman is in her element and has thus discarded the trappings of culture, whereas the man, by retaining them, remains separate, physically and mentally, from the natural world. She is presented as instinctual, he rational. There is a further ambiguity about the naked women in such pictures: they may be interpreted not as real women but as muses, or personifications of man's inspiration in the landscape.

The most obvious scenario uniting naked woman with clothed man is that of the artist with his model; indoors or out it is understood that woman/nature is to be transformed into art/culture through the agency of man the creator. Both are equally passive subject matter recreated by male potency as art. This analogy is obvious in Courbet's *The Artist's Studio* where the naked model looks over the artist's shoulder as he paints a landscape – she is both his muse, the spirit of nature and a symbol of his libido, the sexual energy channelled into creativity. One thinks also of Renoir's voluptuous bathers in the light of his remark 'I paint with my prick' and Van Gogh praising the 'male potency' of Cézanne's work. Artist and naked model pictures emphasize the view that woman's creativity is natural, instinctual (i.e. bearing children, which, it is argued, satisfies and supersedes all other urges to create; an argument used by male critics to explain the lack of any great female artists), whereas man's is artificial, cultural, transcending nature. As Barbara Kruger puts it, in an image of a man's hand drawing a girl's head, 'Your creation is divine our reproduction is human'.

A further category of pictures featuring clothed man and naked woman show rescuer and rescued, hero and victim, again a gendered division. Such subjects seem to have had a particular appeal in the nineteenth century, using the demands of the narrative to excuse and validate the nudity (as today the actress or director will defend nudity on film as 'integral to the story') in a clear-cut moral context. Favourite versions of this theme are *Angelica saved by Ruggiero* (Ingres), St George (*The Knight Errant*) (Millais), and *Perseus and Andromeda* (Burne-Jones). These pictures set up a range of oppositions: the armoured male figure active, hard, invulnerable, a representative of culture, against the naked female, soft, vulnerable, unprotected, as representative of nature.

There is of course an alternative view. The identification of woman with nature offers only a partial account and one can argue for the opposite view (though there is less *visual* evidence to support it). After all, the sensual and nurturing qualities represent only one aspect of nature. It is also characterized as forceful, bloody, 'red in tooth and claw', indiscriminate and uncontrollable while woman can be seen as the product of culture – tamed, domestic, civilized, controlled. The mythology of the artist in Romantic tradition, for instance, presents him as in some sense 'outside' society, accorded a certain licence to ignore its rules and thus closer to a primitive and 'natural' state.

GRAVELOT & COCHIN
Nature 1768 from
Almanach Iconologique
1766–74
Engraving
(British Library, London)

The naked woman has traditionally been the symbol of nature. A beneficent mother of all, a type of Eve before the Fall, surrounded by docile animals and a fertile landscape. Nakedness has always represented wildness, a state outside civilization and culture.

Milk leaks from her breasts, a symbol of nature's life-giving nurturing role. A figure of Diana of Ephesus is to be seen in the background.

SIMON VOUET (1590–1649)
Ceres and Harvesting Cupids
Oil on canvas
(The National Gallery, London)

An ample, naked woman in a ripe and burgeoning landscape, Ceres, goddess of fertility, is symbolic of nature's bounty and nurturing capacity.

JEAN-FRANÇOIS MILLET (1814–75)
Nude girl sitting in a wood
Black chalk

ANNIE W. BRIGMAN (1869–1950)
Soul of the Blasted Pine (detail) 1907
Photogravure
(Royal Photographic Society, Bath)

Brigman chooses to depict herself naked
in the landscape, a traditional
embodiment of the *genius loci*. Imogen
Cunningham (1883–1976), in her lyrical
studies of her husband Roi on Mount
Rainier, Seattle, hijacked this imagery
to demonstrate the existence of an equal
rapport between man and nature. More
recently, Japanese photographer Hiro
Sato has chosen to present his naked
self in orgasmic unity with the natural
world.

WILLIAM ETTY (1787–1849)
The Deluge
Oil on canvas

A rather puzzling picture, perhaps referring to women's sexuality as a cause of the Flood, as of the Fall. It belongs to a great series of pictures in the nineteenth century associating the naked woman with water as a symbol of her sensuality. A transitional element between earth and air, water was, for the ancients, a female principle symbolizing birth and fertility, hence the mythology of Venus (goddess of love) rising from the waves.

WILLIAM ETTY (1787–1849)
Study of a nude female seated on a bank
Watercolour

Etty's anonymous female bather is
descended from the Dianas of Boucher
and others, but even the pretence of a
mythological context to 'explain' the
presence of a female nude in the
landscape has been abandoned here.

ANONYMOUS: ITALIAN 17C
Apollo and Daphne
Oil on canvas

In the story of Apollo and Daphne, we
have the perfect example of active male
sexuality in pursuit of the female. To
escape his assault she is changed,
literally, into a part of nature, in the
form of a laurel tree.

BRASSAI (b.1899)
Untitled image from *Minotaure* 1933
Photograph

The analogies between the curves of the
female body and the forms of the
landscape are drawn in this surrealistic
trick picture in which two torsos create
the illusion of a landscape subject.

BILL BRANDT (1904–83)
Nude
Gelatin silver print

Brandt created a whole series which
projects the female as a natural object
within the landscape. In form and
texture the body is compared and
contrasted with rock, cliff and sand
dune; without other referents this
sculptural form becomes monumental,
fossilized, totally divorced from human
flesh.

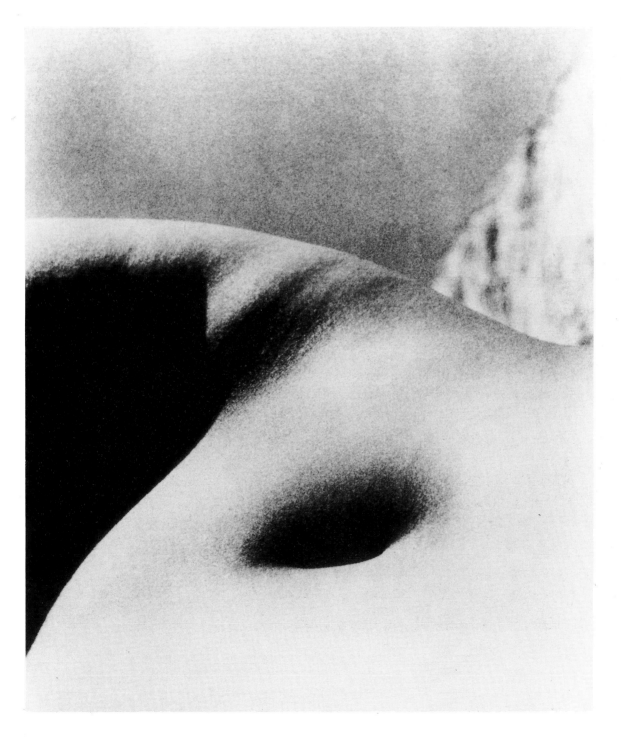

EDWARD WESTON (1886–1958)
Nude 1936
Gelatin silver print

EDWARD WESTON (1886–1958)
Nude floating 1939
Gelatin silver print

ALFRED LYS BALDRY (1858–?)
Two semi-naked girls seated on the
seashore
Platinum print

ALPHONSE LEGROS (1837–1911)
Two studies of a nude female figure,
studies for *La Source* 1882
Pencil

PIERRE-AUGUSTE RENOIR (1841–1919)
La Nymphe de la Source
Oil on canvas
(The National Gallery, London)

The naked female is seen here in her
mythological role as the 'spirit of place',
but also inherent in the personification
as 'La Source' is the analogy between
the spring, a source of life-giving water,
and woman herself as universal mother,
the source of human life. The subject
became almost a cliché within the genre
of the female nude (see also Ingres's
La Source (Louvre) and Courbet's
La Source (Louvre)).

TERRY DENNETT (b.1938) and
JO SPENCE (b.1934)
Subordination (from *Remodelling
Photo-History*) 1982
Gelatin silver print
(Courtesy of the artists)

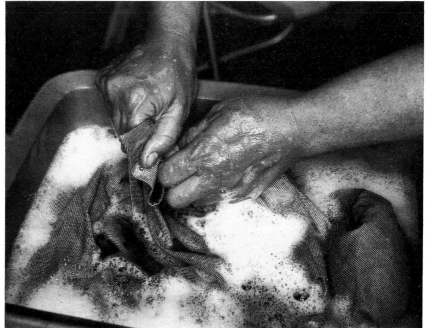

GIORGIONE (*c.*1476/8–1510)
Concert Champêtre
Oil on canvas
(Musées Nationaux, Paris)

PABLO PICASSO (1881–1973)
Nude under a pine tree (Femme nue sous
un pin) 1959
Oil on canvas, 182.9 × 244 cm
(Grant J. Pick Collection, 1965. 687,
©1988 The Art Institute of Chicago,
All Rights Reserved)

Painted in earth tones, the woman is
monumental, the curves of her reclining
form analogous to the line of the hills
behind her. Her body is spread out for
us like a map, like a bird's-eye view of a
landscape.

ÉDOUARD MANET (1832–83)
Le Déjeuner sur l'Herbe
Oil on canvas
(Courtauld Institute Galleries, London
(Courtauld Collection))

SIR WILLIAM ORPEN (1878–1931)
The draughtsman and his model 1911
Watercolour

Woman is represented here as muse,
allied by her nakedness to nature while
her clothed male companions represent
culture. Orpen's picture with its male
artist and female model in a landscape
setting, draws together many of the
themes already discussed. She is naked
but for her necklace, her hair loose, and
hiding her face as she droops her head
down. Her pose suggests both weariness
(working as an artist's model is a
strenuous and tiring business) and shame
at her nakedness in the face of his intense
scrutiny.

KARL SCHMIDT-ROTTLUFF (1884–1976)
Self-portrait I 1913
Woodcut

Though this is designated a self-portrait, the artist himself is compressed into the upper left-hand corner of the frame, from where he peers over the shoulder of a naked woman (model/mistress) whose figure dominates the composition. The dominance of the female nude leads us to assume that the artist wishes to present himself and his creative powers in terms of his sexual potency, his libido, as symbolized by the available, submissive, naked woman. He grasps her proprietorially but also to display her nakedness to the viewer. Her eyes are averted, as if ashamed or uncomfortable with her position. She fills the frame but is anonymous; he presents her as the product of his creative powers so that she forms part of *his* identity.

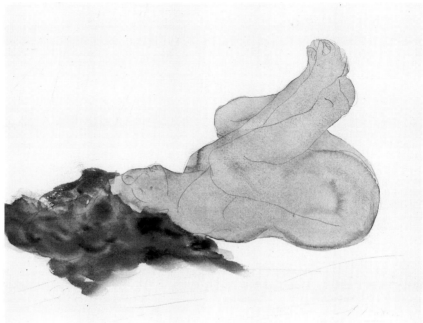

FORMERLY ATTRIBUTED TO AUGUSTE RODIN (1840–1917)
Study of a nude female figure, lying on her back with her hands clasping her feet
Pencil and watercolour

Rodin, like Renoir, Picasso and Courbet, made explicit in his life and work the connections between his libido and his subject matter (his lover, Gwen John, also served him as a model), the naked female body. In later life he produced several series of drawings and watercolour sketches of female nudes, contorted and blatantly displaying breasts and genitals. For him, a woman's nakedness was a 'natural' condition and she herself a part of nature, raw material for the artist:

'By following Nature one obtains everything. When I have a beautiful woman's body as a model, the drawings I make of it also give me pictures of insects, birds and fishes . . . A woman, a mountain or a horse are formed according to the same principles.' (Quoted in *Henry Moore: Sculpture and Drawings 1921–48* Vol.I, Edited by David Sylvester, London 1957.)

GUSTAVE COURBET (1819–77)
The Painter's Studio (detail) 1855
Oil on canvas
(Musées Nationaux, Paris)

Compare this with the pictures on
pp.111–12.

PABLO PICASSO (1881–1973)
Sculpteur, Modèle couché et Sculpture
1933
Etching

The artist/sculptor gazes at his sculpture which responds with a challenging stare and the confrontation of a phallic stave (he is thus presented as a kind of alter ego). The female model is draped across the artist's lap, clearly defined as his libido/inspiration but passive, not a part of the relationship between the artist and his work.

FRANZ FIEDLER (n.d.)
The Artist 1930
Bromoil
(Royal Photographic Society, Bath)

He confronts the camera and the model, confident, comfortable, in control. She is anonymous, her body displayed to him.

BRASSAI (b.1899)
Matisse with his model
Gelatin silver print

He looks at her; her gaze is averted, downcast; her pose is designed to display her body. She is associated with the painting on the left of the composition, within which we see a painted female nude. This model, too, will be recreated as 'art', as a product of 'culture' by the analytic male intelligence. She is the subject of art, he is the creator who will transform her.

Matisse voices the unconscious egotism of man the creator who transcends the imperfections, even the presence, of the model:

'For me nature is always present. As in love, all depends on what the artist unconsciously projects on everything he sees. It is the quality of that projection, rather than the presence of a living

person, that gives an artist's vision its life.' (Quoted in Lawrence Gowing, *Matisse* (London, 1979))

This is tantamount to an admission that woman, as an object of love or of art, is no more than a blank anonymous screen on which the lover/artist projects his fantasies.

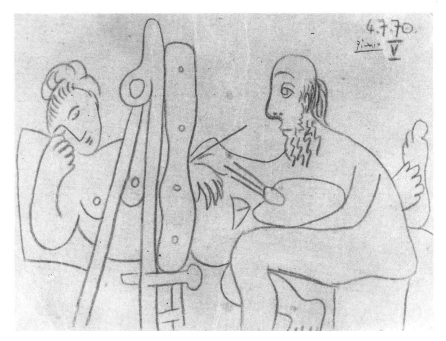

PABLO PICASSO (1887–1973)
Le Peintre et Son Modèle (V)
Coloured pencil on cardboard
(Musée National d'Art Moderne, Paris)

In all of Picasso's artist/model pictures, the male figure dominates, aggressively phallic, larger, darker, and angular against the rounded forms of the female. His palette and brushes are wielded unmistakably as phallic symbols; they indicate that the violent eroticism of these pictures is a substitute for sex. This is painting as creative act, generative, possessive, violating the naked woman in paint as in passion.

In this particular image the woman lies prone, bisected by the easel, her sex clearly defined and displayed to the artist. He sits upright, active and in control. Effectively nothing has changed in the relationship between artist (male) and naked model (female) in the 400 years since Dürer's *Draughtsman drawing a nude* (see p.30).

SIR JOHN EVERETT MILLAIS (1829–96)
The Knight Errant
Oil on canvas
(The Tate Gallery, London)

JEAN-AUGUSTE-DOMINIQUE INGRES
(1780–1867)
Angelica saved by Ruggiero
Oil on canvas
(The National Gallery, London)

Such scenes create a series of gendered
oppositions which set up man
as representative of culture, woman as
representative of nature. He is
armoured, invulnerable, active, while
she, naked, is passive, vulnerable,
unprotected. Such images demonstrate
the power of culture over nature.

NEW DIRECTIONS?

Representation of the world, like the world itself, is the
work of men; they describe it from their own point of
view which they confuse with the absolute truth.

Simone de Beauvoir, *The Second Sex*, 1972

The representation of the female nude has long been the prerogative of men. Not only was the control and possession of female sexuality mediated through images of the nude, but women were excluded from the life class because it formed part of the male hegemony of high culture (in Zoffany's picture of the founder members of the Royal Academy Angelica Kauffmann and Mary Moser are represented by their portraits to avoid the impropriety of showing women in the presence of the male life model.) Women's admittance to the life class coincided with the beginnings of the decline of life-drawing as a major feature of an academic fine-art training. And now that there are no moral or social restraints on women artists wishing to work with the nude the discipline has been further devalued by ceasing to be a compulsory feature on the curriculum of most art schools.

Though women could and did paint the female nude (it being more readily accessible to them than the male) examples are rare and remarkable to the extent that authorship is often disputed. The modesty proper to the female sex in a patriarchal society led to misattributions such as Artemisia Gentileschi's *Susanna* to her father Orazio.[12] Even now, as was seen in reactions to the 1982 ICA exhibition 'Women's Images of Men' entrenched opinion cannot give an impartial assessment of nudes by women. Perhaps this is indicative of a certain resentment, a feeling that women are trespassing on what has been regarded as a male preserve. For centuries representations of the female nude have been constructed by men. The female nude was devised as a category of secular art with no purpose beyond the more or less erotic depiction of nakedness. The Judgement of Paris as a subject in painting is a case in point; it very early lost its mythic significance as an explanation of events leading to the Trojan war, becoming merely an excuse to display naked female beauty for male delectation. The female nude did not appear in Greek sculpture until the fifth century BC when she had been purged of her original eastern associations with fertility and childbirth. In other words she was not acceptable to a patriarchal society until she had been reduced to an object of sexual desire. Throughout its history the image of the female nude has been emptied of women's experience, to be used by men as the expression of their own sexuality. Of course, male artists and critics have always justified their enjoyment of the nude and its validity as a genre by appealing to abstract conceptions of ideal form, beauty and aesthetic value. Thus women who object to images of the nude, whatever the context or the message, are castigated as philistines and prudes (as was Labour MP Clare Short over her recent campaign to ban photographs of the topless Page 3 girl from the tabloid newspapers), and their very real discomfort dismissed. But even Kenneth Clark, who typifies the connoisseur's approach to the nude, revealed the underlying attitude of the male to images of the naked female when he said that 'no nude, however abstract, should fail to arouse in the spectator some vestige of erotic feeling – and if it does not do so, it is bad art and false morals.'[13]

Essentially women have been alienated from their own image since it is presented to them in a form which allows them only two options; a narcissistic appreciation or a heightened sense of vulnerability and discomfort. As Mary Kelly has said: 'I think when we're looking at images of women, for both men and women, we are voyeurs, we're pleasurably involved in that looking, but I think something different happens to the woman. She's in some way troubled by the kinds of identification that she makes with her image.'[14]

Faced with images which set up female sexuality as reactive, narcissistic and exhibitionist, and the female body as occupied territory in culture and in nature (pregnancy), women artists are attempting to retrieve the nude and to infuse it with specifically personal and feminist meanings. Like Mary Daly, in her work on language, customs, culture and history, women are searching for ways to remake and to re-present their own naked image free of patriarchal and phallic associations. As Lisa Tickner has said, 'the colonized territory must be reclaimed from masculine fantasy, the "lost" aspects of female body experience authenticated and re-integrated in opposition to its more familiar and seductive artistic role as raw material for the men.'[15]

Women artists who wish to challenge the existing stereotypes of the female nude as erotic spectacle are using a variety of strategies: the reworking of myths, the deconstruction of dominant visual codes, parody, role-reversal, and the re-presentation of specifically female body experience and imagery. There has been some resistance from women to the idea of using their own bodies in art because they were reluctant to submit to the historical emphasis on women's bodies as sex objects. Certain feminist critics have seen this use of body imagery as dangerous in that it continues the traditional polarization of woman/nature (body) and man/culture (mind): 'But in celebrating what is essentially female we may simply be re-inforcing oppressive definitions of women, e.g. women as always in their separate sphere, or women as defining their identities exclusively, and narcissistically, through their bodies.'[16]

Indeed the depiction of the nude by women in a form intended to parody or subvert the sexist or pornographic image almost invariably fails. The more attractive the artist/model, the greater the danger that her naked image will be misappropriated, easily assimilated, by a male audience, to those images she is seeking to undermine. A case in point is the exhibition advertisement by Lynda Benglis in *Artforum* (1974), featuring herself naked and gesticulating with a large rubber dildo. This self-portrait with its attempt to assimilate male energy in the symbolic form of the phallus, collapses into ambiguity and confusion because the form is too close to that which it seeks to parody, and Benglis herself with her lithe oiled body is indistinguishable from the stereotype of male fantasy, her aggressive self-awareness synonymous with provocative teasing, the classic 'come-on'.

Carolee Schneeman, a sixties performance artist who often appeared naked, explained her use of nudity thus: 'In some sense I made a gift of my body to other women: giving our bodies back to ourselves. The haunting images of Cretan bull dancers – joyful, free, bare-breasted, skilled women leaping precisely from danger to ascendency, guided my imagination.'[17]

This positive and optimistic approach is characteristic of the 1960s and 1970s but women have been increasingly aware that, as Lucy Lippard observed, 'It is a subtle abyss that separates men's use of women for sexual titillation from women's use of women to expose that insult.'[18] Awareness of this danger has led most of the women artists working with the nude to use their own bodies as subject and by so doing they escaped the traditional artist/model subject/object relationship, using the body as a locus in which art and artist are interchangeable. The use of one's own body is inevitable when the aim is to explore the relationship between individual experience and the social construction of femininity; at the same time it avoids, or tempers, the accusations of exploitation which surround man-made images of the female nude in feminist criticism.

The male nude is comparatively rare in women's art, presumably from a lack of interest or response to images of the naked male body. Nude male pin-ups in the magazines *Cosmopolitan* and *Viva* were soon abandoned and *Playgirl* survives on a readership composed largely of male homosexuals. As yet the social construct of women's sexuality does not accommodate a relation to such images, and very few artists have attempted to offer new ways of presenting the male nude. The role reversal of women gazing at a man, which seems automatically to render him passive, is not comfortable or convincing for an audience of either sex and demonstrates the impossibility of changing entrenched social relations by force. Whatever the message it carries, the female nude is ultimately less controversial, more acceptable in our society; she can be associated with the countless media images of naked women which range from pornography, and the ubiquitous Page 3 girl, through fashion photography and advertisements to film and fine art. But these nudes, which are commonplace in popular culture, are either sanitized and censored, or blatantly provocative, whereas women's use of the nude has attempted to de-eroticize it (or to make it expressive of women's experience of sexuality) by challenging its male-imposed taboos, and instead emphasizing the rhythms and changes of fertility and childbirth, the biological functions of the body rather than the purely sexual aspects.

In many ways the female nude is a natural and inevitable subject for the woman artist; women have a stronger awareness of their bodies than men: their physical cycles are more insistent, and they have been conditioned by society's definitions of femininity to treat their bodies as 'raw material for manipulation and display'.[19] Advertising imagery is carefully calculated, presenting an 'ideal' face or body for the consumer to emulate by purchasing the product; women are surrounded by icons of perfection which enslave them; witness the way in which the desired body-shape is influenced by male-dictated fashions.[20] For women this body-shape is constantly changing to focus on waist, or legs, or breasts while men retain a natural comfortable silhouette. John Berger sees this emphasis on appearance as governing women's behaviour: 'she has to survey everything she is and everything she does because how she appears to others, and ultimately how she appears to men, is of crucial importance for what is normally thought of as the success of her life. Her own sense of being in herself is supplanted by a sense of being appreciated as herself by another.'[21] Physical desirability has, in the West, been elevated as the crucial factor in sexual relations, and in our society desirability is largely signified by appearance, though women, much more than men, are judged on this level alone.

Women's use of their body image in art has been motivated by a desire to retrieve it from the public (i.e. male) domain. Our culture is, even now, saturated with images of the female nude created by men and expressive of male sexuality. Women artists are working with the nude to extend its expressive and symbolic possibilities, and to invest it with an idea of women's experience of sexuality (which in the face of the aggressive male 'look' is often attempting to resist display and definition). Alexis Hunter has explained 'I might refer to the female nude now but she is always active, symbolic of female action, and although painted in a sensual style she is not up for sale, not offered to the viewer.'[22] Feminist art strategies involve breaking taboos surrounding childbirth, menstruaton, vaginal imagery, and celebrating what have hitherto been areas of shame for women and thus weapons of subjugation. Feminism suggests that our experience of the body affects socially-determined psychic processes. By using the nude, women are trying to present this female experience which until very recently has been hidden, and held to be an improper or inappropriate subject for art. For instance pregnancy is rare in art, because it is not an acceptable image of female beauty; vaginal imagery (with the exception of Judy Chicago's feminist celebration *The Dinner Party*, 1974–9) is found only in pornography, and breast-feeding largely disappeared from representations of the Virgin and Child around 1500 (it became indecorous for the Virgin to bare her breast as purity became increasingly allied to modesty) though it continued in the more erotic context of 'Caritas' subjects. Feminism itself has contributed to this concealment of motherhood by devaluing it against the liberation of a career.

Pregnancy and childbirth have been one of the taboos in art, though motherhood has been sanctioned as a right and proper subject since the earliest representations of the Virgin and Child. Thus has a whole central area of women's physical and spiritual experience been excluded from visual representation. The naked pregnant female is controversial in a patriarchal society which has elevated the female nude to a public icon, because she does not conform to the established aesthetic of physical form. (The anti-smoking campaign poster showing a heavily-pregnant woman caused a furore, not because she was smoking but because she was naked. Pregnancy in our society is treated as a private and rather shameful state, part of our ambivalence towards children and to motherhood.)

The climate of openness about women's bodies that was fostered by feminism in the 1970s resulted in several works which examine the experience of pregnancy in visual form. Susan Hiller's series of photographic panels *10 Months* (1977–8) recorded the physical progress of her own pregnancy together with texts which illuminate her state of mind, her preoccupations, throughout its duration. These successive views of the pregnant belly seen prone and in profile were shown alongside examples of the traditional reclining nude (in the show *British Art 1940–1980* at the Hayward Gallery, London, 1980) disrupting the limited and limiting view of the female body. Hiller's images focus on the site of pregnancy; by choosing to isolate a part of the body and presenting it in this way Hiller makes a significant landscape analogy, and in deliberately choosing grainy black-and-white prints acts 'to break with the sentimental image of pregnancy'. The accompanying text celebrates the mental fertility and creative powers that accompanied the physical burgeoning.

Compare these images, which in their relentless sequence of expanding forms, convey some idea of the sensations of pregnancy, with three studies by men: Andrew Williams's *Lateral Colour Map of a Full-Term Primipara Produced by Light* 1977, Barry Lategan's study of his wife pregnant with their son, *Charlene and Dylan*, 1980, and Leonard McComb's *Pregnant Woman*, 1975. Both Williams and Lategan show more of the body than Hiller, but even in a photograph which purports to be a portrait, the head is not shown. Both treat the body as a textured volumetric form, Williams by means of the contour lines, Lategan by having greased his wife's body leaving a pattern of white smears on her dark skin. The male view is necessarily that of an outsider, however intimately connected with the process, and his view is more scientific, detached. But there is a tenderness in Lategan's portrait and in McComb's sensitive drawing which bespeaks a new attitude to the female nude and to women's body experience, an attempt to understand rather than exploit.

Birth itself is very rarely depicted in art but it forms the powerful central focus for Rose Garrard's *Talisman: The Wooden Box From Her Father*, 1988. This is one of a series of twelve drawings based on a 2000-year-old gnostic text celebrating the female principle. Naked but not provocative this matriarchal trio endorses the view of woman as the 'Great Mother' in whose body resides the power of life and death.

Helen Chadwick has used her own naked body for two major projects: in *Ego Geometria Sum* (1984) photographs of her naked body were applied to simple sculptural shapes representing cradle, piano, gym horse etc. to demonstrate how her upbringing (society's rules and expectations) have moulded and restricted her. The nudity is expressive of innocence, the natural state of childhood before it acquires the veneer of culture. More recently, in *Of Mutability*, she has examined the body as matter. Where the early work charted the body in culture and showed it constrained and struggling, *Of Mutability* allies the body with nature, at once freer, more fluid, vivacious, acrobatic. Here Chadwick reinforces the woman/nature analogy using nakedness to suggest the body in its elemental state. The figure has discarded the paraphernalia of culture, retaining only the ornaments which accentuate her nakedness. Like the wise women, the so-called witches, she presents herself as an instinctual part of the natural world, in sympathy with plants and animals. Defending her use of the nude Chadwick has said: 'Progress has to be made through self-understanding, self-awareness, but one of the taboos has been an exploration of one's own body.'[23] This has been one of the most fundamental taboos challenged by feminism; in the early days of the women's movement consciousness-raising was augmented by sessions involving self-examination of the vagina, and the book *Our Bodies Ourselves*[24] became the bible of the newly-liberated woman. In the *Of Mutability* installation Chadwick presents woman stripped of cultural identity and thus free of social restraints, free to reinvent herself to fulfil her physical and sexual potential.

In *One Flesh* she uses the body of a friend and her new-born baby girl to confront the Madonna myth and a phallocentric Christianity pointed up by the mother's gesture to the child's sex. Chadwick takes the sanitized image of the Madonna and reveals that the birth experience, which is, after all, her transcendent function, involves blood and pain; she wears a red cloak, rather than the spiritual blue usually associated with the Virgin. The emphasis is on the physical experience of childbirth – the umbilical cord, the placenta, the ring-adorned labia, and the breasts, reinstated to their proper role in motherhood. The nursing mother is still very largely taboo in our society, and effectively banned from public places, and her representation in art, even in Virgin and Child subjects, is rarer still. In our culture the display of the breast is acceptable only in a sexual context (Desmond Morris and other male anthropologists have explained the development of the female hominid breast as a sexual signal, ignoring its real biological function). Above all, *One Flesh* celebrates the 'hidden' sexual bond between mother and child; they are literally 'one flesh', united by the umbilical cord, and figuratively, by sharing the same gender. Chadwick is thus suggesting an alternative sexual fulfilment to that set out in Genesis 2:24: 'Therefore a man leaves his father and his mother and cleaves to his woman and they become one flesh'.

Certain feminist writers, most notably Susan Griffin and Adrienne Rich, have swum against the tide of feminist thought (which seeks to dissolve difference) to claim nature as the female sphere. Rich asserts that women must 'think through the body'[25] Griffin that women must express 'what is still wild in us'.[26] The painter Eileen Cooper offers the visual embodiment of this view. Cooper has frankly accepted, even welcomed, the traditional nurturing role, offering a vibrant celebration of motherhood and its pleasures, but showing it as active rather than passive. Woman as the Great Mother dominates these pictures, a naked life-giving goddess. Cooper's imagery and narratives are drawn from her own life, and of late specifically her role as mother, and in that sense her nudes are self-portraits. Nakedness is not the subject of Cooper's pictures, it is an incidental: thus we see that these figures are both archetypes and herself. The woman's elemental nakedness places her firmly in the sphere of nature where she is an active participant, digging, planting, tending, nurturing, so at one with the natural world that birds perch on her, insects crawl over her, fish submit to her caress. In these images woman is the creator while man is reduced to bystander, a passive scarecrow or child-minding father. Woman is the life-force from whom all blessings flow and the sign of her power is her nakedness.

Gwen Hardie, too, in her most recent images of the female nude, is presenting an archetype, a pictograph of the body. The earlier work – monumental heads, fists, breasts – offered an intense physicality heightened by the tactile quality of the sponged paint. These were not provocative or in any way assimilable to the man-made tradition of fragmenting the female body. Usually self-portraits, these close-ups offered the body as source of power and energy, their massive scale suggesting the disproportionate significance of the body in both visual and psychic discourse. Hardie's latest work offers the embodiment of Barbara Hepworth's remark: 'body experience is the centre of creation. I rarely draw what I see. I draw what I feel in my body.' These new pictures show woman's experience of her body as centred on the reproductive organs, the menstrual cycle. In primitivist diagrammatic form Hardie seeks to make visible, to emphasize, the pyschic significance of the female genitalia which the dominant phallocentric male view of the female body has hidden, ignored or misunderstood. These bodies are not erotic; they lack the physicality of the images that preceded them in Hardie's *œuvre*. Rather, they arise from her discovery that 'for the first time I understood painting as a construction of an idea, rather than a study of the object in space'.

Jacqueline Morreau and Alexis Hunter have worked to re-interpret myths and to reinstate mythic heroines, characters such as Pandora, Eve, Psyche, who have been cast as 'bad' by patriarchy. They have been falsely defined solely as sources of evil, or as *femmes fatales*, exploiting their fair nakedness to beguile men and unleash miseries on the world. All were guilty of curiosity – 'scientific enquiry' in a man, but sinful in a woman. These figures, almost always represented naked, as a sign of their sexuality and their sinfulness, articulate the complex of associations in patriarchal society between woman, sexuality and death. Instead both Morreau and Hunter offer positive models for women by uncovering meanings suppressed or distorted in conventional interpretations. In her triptych *Persephone* Morreau celebrates the mother/daughter bond, and shows it to be as powerful as that between a woman and her lover. Usually reduced to a rape or abduction, the Persephone myth in fact explores women's ambivalence towards men and to the consequences of their own fertility.

Roberta Graham's work has explored the connections between woman, sex and death. For Graham the expression of sexuality involves sacrifice, an annihilation of self in an erotic ecstasy of communion. The death of the self, and death as inevitable concomitant of love (and of birth, as we see in the *Fallen Angel* cycle) is pointed up by Graham: in *L'Amour/La Mort* she literally tears out her heart for her lover, offering her death with her love. In *Life Sighs in Sleep* the naked female figure is transparent, the skeleton showing through the skin; death is prefigured in the sensual post-coital abandon of this figure.

Graham's work aims at a rehabilitation of eroticism, and of vulnerability for women *and* men. She uses her own naked body and the bodies of male collaborators in photography and performance to explore the expression of

HELEN CHADWICK (b.1953)
One Flesh
Colour photocopy

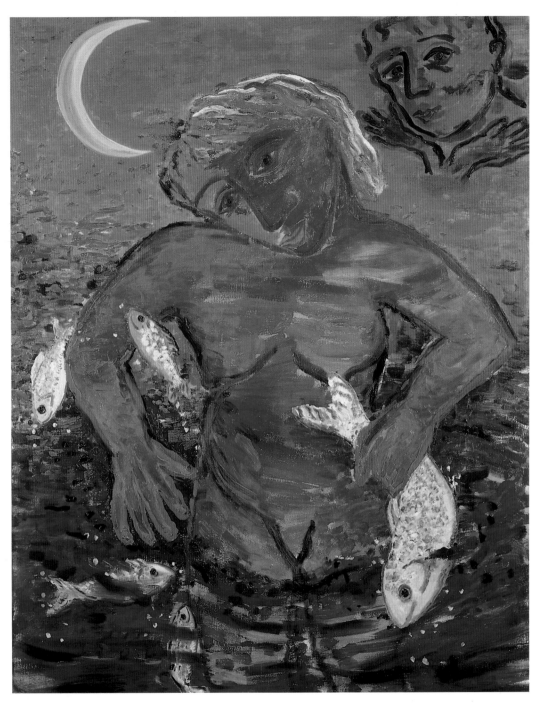

EILEEN COOPER (b.1953)
Tickling the Trout 1987
Oil on canvas
(Private Collection, London
Photograph courtesy of the artist,
c/o The Benjamin Rhodes Gallery,
London)

GWEN HARDIE (b.1962)
Venus with Spikes 1986
Oil on canvas
(Gulbenkian Foundation, Lisbon)

Hardie takes Venus, the archetypal male fantasy, the goddess of love, and invests her with the realities of female body experience. Her spikes are turned in upon herself, like that instrument of torture, the Iron Maiden: they symbolize the psychic pains, the physical torments inflicted upon women by their bodies and by a phallocentric society's emphasis on body image, the ideal versus the real. In the tradition of the early Christian martyrs, women have been inculcated with a fear and shame of their bodies. The burdensome flesh is subject to mortification/mutilation in the form of dieting (leading to bulimia, anorexia and concomitant amenorrhoea (loss of periods and thus of true adult sexuality)), exercise, surgery, drugs, bleaching, waxing, electrolysis, the swallowing of hormones or insertion of contraceptive devices. It is no accident that this primitive schema of the female body is dominated by the oestral parts; this, for women is part of the reality of female sexuality. Pregnancy is, even now, an inevitable corollary of the sexual act, desired or dreaded, possible or impossible, actual or potential.

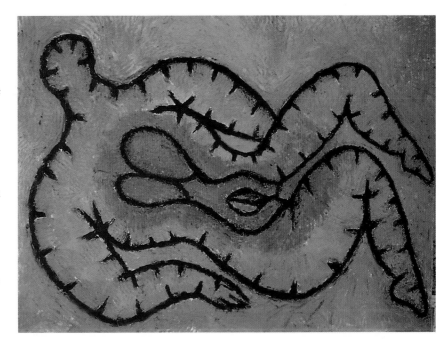

JEFFERY CAMP (b.1923)
Tower Bridge 1985
Oil on canvas
(Nigel Greenwood Gallery, London)

ALEXIS HUNTER (b.1948)
The Sound of the Moon
Acrylic on paper
(Sargent Gallery, Wanganui,
New Zealand)

The naked woman listens to her body, to her menstrual cycle (which is in turn linked to the phases of the moon).

Hunter emphasizes the importance of recognizing the body's rhythms rather than denying them. Menstruation, traditionally shameful and secret, and in many societies hedged around with taboos, is here shown to be natural.

vulnerability. Despite this, feminist criticism has attacked her work as being open to appropriation by men, her women allegedly too sensual – the abandoned pose of the figure (herself) in *Life Sighs in Sleep* was admittedly taken from pictures of Marilyn Monroe and from historical nudes – offering the female body too readily as a site/sight of pleasure. But Graham's women are neither submissive nor vulnerable in the manner of conventional nudes produced by men. They are autonomous, powerful, giving, their nakedness itself a disguise to be torn aside to disclose heart, muscles, veins, skeleton. She shows us real women of flesh and blood literally casting off the constricting identity that nudity imposes upon them.

Fallen Angel, inspired by the life of Mary Shelley, is a complex many-layered piece reflecting Graham's preoccupation with the connections between birth, death and sex. Shelley suffered a near-fatal miscarriage, and the early deaths of several children. The hopes and fears, the physical and mental traumas surrounding childbirth are expressed through Graham's impersonation of Shelley. But in focusing on women's bodies and experiences Graham aims to be neither separatist nor divisive; she advocates a holistic philosophy based on a union of opposites. In panel 7 of *Fallen Angel* she is transformed into a two-headed hermaphrodite as a protest against the separation of experience into 'male' and 'female' spheres. The Bible says of Adam and Eve 'male and female created he them', an ambiguous form that suggests the existence of a pre-lapsarian androgynous unity. Indeed William Blake saw the tragedy of the Fall in the fact that 'The Feminine separates from the Masculine', the ideal of androgynous harmony disrupted by discord and division.

Jeffery Camp offers a similarly positive view of relations between the sexes in his slender androgynous nudes. Camp ascribes the same qualities to his models without distinction between male and female: 'The people I have drawn have been inspiring, beautiful, vital, elegant, innocent, desirable, patient, sensuous and strong.' Camp unites active and passive, nature and culture; the so-called 'sprung' figure (female) is both active and vulnerable, passive yet strong and vigorous. There is an elemental *joie de vivre* about these couples as they recline in an aura of post-coital tenderness (*Falling Snow, Hastings*, 1983; *Tower Bridge*, 1985) or as they plunge dizzyingly into the vortex of passion (*Rocket Over Venice*, 1986). For Camp 'A man and woman together are charged with a sympathetic force' and he finds hope in the willingness to embrace a 'naked vulnerability'. His nudes are pure embodiments of the ideal of androgyny in terms of balance, equality, harmony.

In spite of the revival of figurative painting in the 1980s women seeking to disrupt the stereotypes of the nude have worked almost exclusively with photography and other 'new' media. Painting and drawing are burdened with a history of meanings, uses and associations, and a painting of a naked woman intended to celebrate women's sexuality can be more easily appropriated by the voyeuristic tradition of the female nude. The technological media are untainted by the burdens of historicism and by using them the artist cuts across existing representational hierarchies.

But even photography has now been contaminated with patriarchal definitions resulting from its use in pornography and in advertising. An artist such as Sue Arrowsmith bypasses such associations by manipulating the process, or over-painting photographic images. In *Against Interpretation* she takes one of the icons of our culture, an archetype of female nudity, the *Venus de Milo*, and sets up a figure to approximate its pose. This damaged and damaging symbol of female beauty is, in three of the panels, partially obscured by crude brush strokes which veil the image and enable it literally to defy interpretation. It attempts to escape the imposed definitions of a patriarchal culture (where 'meaning is masculine'[27]) which limits and restricts possibilities of female self-determination. *One, Two, Three: Nine* tackles the stereotype of the naked woman. Nine images are created by direct contact of the body on light-sensitive paper. The body is constrained, limited, pigeonholed by these boxes which thus represent the definitions of woman's role and the character of female nudity which society imposes. The bodies struggle against their confines, with gestures pushing outwards against the viewer and poses that resist and deflect the male gaze, resisting definition and possession. Arrowsmith thus successfully reclaims the nude so as to represent female experience rather than male fantasy, but in order to do this she has had to mask and obscure the image, the nudity being suggested rather than being presented in graphic detail.

Men using their own naked bodies in their art, are, by contrast, rare (Stanley Spencer, John Coplans, various performance artists). Men have no need to explore their own body image because their relation to the world is not mediated through the body in the same way. Joe Gantz has featured as a player in his own improvised encounters between men and women, often naked (*Men Swearing Fidelity*, *The Little Soldier*) but his most recent work, in which nudity is foregrounded, has concentrated exclusively on the female body.

A series of female nudes, *The Possibility for Love*,[28] resulted from a collaboration between photographer and models; each image shows a single female figure in a formal emblematic pose. These images have been interpreted as an attempt to confront the 'bad' associations attached to representations of the naked female body – passive, acquiescent, adorned – and to substitute new positive interpretations, but few women, faced with these photographs, can fail to feel a sense of unease. Whatever the circumstances of the production of these photographs they are hard to read as images of female sexuality offered willingly. The potential for a positive reading – women powerful, confident, assertive, neither flirtatious nor ashamed – are undercut by a closer analysis of their styling. The bodies appear as passive manipulated objects, each adorned to emphasize the sexual characteristics: vagina, nipples, and mouth are crudely outlined with red pigment, finger and toenails are painted red (a time-honoured sign of woman as leisured sex-object). Ribbons hobble ankles, and are tied across mouths: woman giftwrapped (*Gift From God; I'm Yours Always*) but bearing overtones of bondage and constraint, of silencing objections and thwarting self-determination. All have eyes closed or heads veiled, blind to their predicament (but then 'love is blind'). On the evidence of these photographs, it would seem that for Gantz, the 'possibility for love' depends on maintenance of the status quo: a woman's passivity and collusion in presenting herself as sexual spectable.

Women artists are, as we have seen, employing a variety of strategies to disrupt the traditional signification of the female nude; male artists such as Gantz are still using the naked woman solely as a sign and object of male desire, yet attempting to persuade us that this position is both valid and desirable for women too. Gantz is only the most honest example of this view; one can also cite the painters David Salle, Eric Fischl, John Stezaker. Fischl's naked women are threatening manifestations of the 'other', possessing a 'caged sexual ferociousness'.[29] Salle's spread-eagled nudes are lifted from pornographic magazines. While the deliberately poor painting and the crude outline drawing emphasize the emptiness and banality of their originals, they nevertheless accept and validate this two-dimensional view of women's bodies as the focus of men's desire, passive objects lacking dignity or autonomy. John Stezaker's headless nudes, thinly screen-printed on silk, use the female body as object or cipher; the frieze-like composition *Veils* is fetishistic in its rhythmic repetition, the naked headless body a seductively-flexed Salome.

The male nude continues to be conspicuous by its absence – even in photography where it makes its most frequent appearance, its purpose is largely formal, offering no real challenge to existing readings of the male body (with the exception of some attempts to re-present it as an object of contemplation/appreciation in the tradition of the female nude). The female nude thus remains the site of discourse about the body. As Mary Kelly has said: 'Definitions of women's femininity are constructed primarily on the body: in the procreative capacity and as fetishized object – to be looked at.' Women are caught between two conflicting ideologies, both founded on male control and definition of female sexuality. On the one hand there is the pressure to conform to the male ideal of display and availability in order to function in society, and at the same time society expresses its fear of women's sexuality by teaching women to be ashamed of their bodies, to regard them as both sinful and imperfect.

Women artists are working with the nude to show that display need not equal availability, that the experience of the female body is not invalidated by imperfection (see Jo Spence's investigations, via photo-therapy, of the body in relation to psychic wellbeing) and are exploring ways of reinvesting the nude with a sense of women's experience of sex and the body that is censored or expunged in men's images of the female nude. Different strategies have emerged to achieve this, ranging from manipulated figuration (Chadwick) through the creation of archetypes (Cooper, Hardie), to the veiling of the figure (Arrowsmith). All have concluded that the tradition of literal figuration has been contaminated beyond retrieval; if the nude is to be the medium for the expression of woman's experience, woman's desire, it must be reconstructed, repictured, in images which refuse definition, resist a literal interpretation. As Chadwick said of her installation *Of Mutability*, 'The issue of the female body as the site of desire is deeply problematic because of the way it has been historically appropriated and colonised . . . The whole work is like a mirror to yourself, trying to know the unknowable. Which is desire.'[30]

RICHARD EARLOM (1743–1822) AFTER
JOHANN ZOFFANY (1733–1810)
The Academicians of the Royal Academy
1773
Mezzotint

SIX/ She speaks (as a woman) about everything, although
they wish her to speak only about women's things. They
like her to speak about everything only if she does not
speak ''as a woman'', only if she will agree in advance to
play the artist's role as neutral (neuter) observor.

She does not speak (as a woman) about anything, although
they want her to. There is nothing she can speak of ''as a
woman''. As a woman, she can not speak.

SUSAN HILLER (b.1941)
10 months (six) (detail) 1977–8
Photographs
(Collection: Arts Council of Great
Britain and Art Gallery of South
Australia, Adelaide)

ANDREW WILLIAMS (b.1952)
*Lateral Colour Map of a Full-Term
Primipara Produced by Light* 1977
Kodak Transfer paper, toned with
colour centre dye
(Collection: Arts Council of Great
Britain)

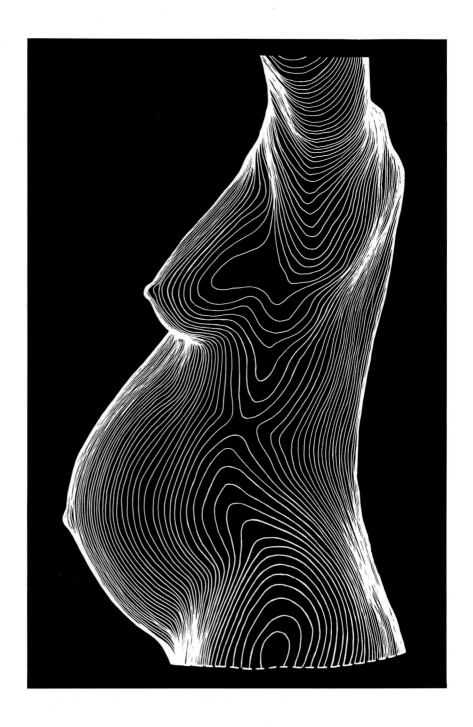

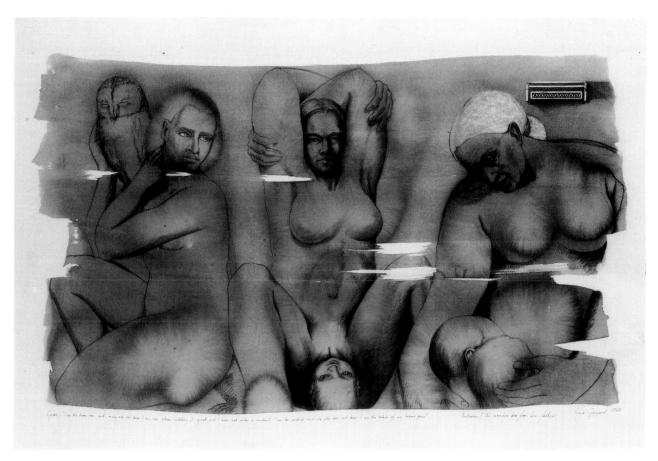

ROSE GARRARD (b.1946)
*Talisman: The Wooden Box From Her
Father* 1988
Acrylic and wash on paper

One of a series of twelve drawings based
on meditations on a 2,000-year-old
gnostic text, *The Thunder, Perfect Mind*,
which was rediscovered in 1946. The
text, which is spoken by a female voice
in the first person, is that of the female
principle within the spiritual Godhead.

HELEN CHADWICK (b.1953)
Of Mutability (installation) 1986
Photocopy

EILEEN COOPER (b.1953)
The Scarecrow 1987
Oil on canvas
(Photograph courtesy of the artist,
c/o The Benjamin Rhodes Gallery,
London)

ROBERTA M. GRAHAM (b.1954)
The First Cut (detail) 1983 (From
Lumières Noires)
Lightbox/sculpture
(Courtesy of the artist)

SUE ARROWSMITH (b.1950)
Against Interpretation 1986
Seven photographic panels
(Collection: Arts Council of Great
Britain)

By reconstructing an icon of female
beauty in the flesh, Arrowsmith shows
us how culture (art) validates the
objectification of the female body.

SUE ARROWSMITH (b.1950)
One, Two, Three: Nine 1985
Photographic panels
(Courtesy Anthony Reynolds Gallery,
London)

NOTES

1. Frascina and Harrison

2. A reviewer in the *Art Journal*, 1856, said of the central figure in William Edward Frost's *The Graces*, 'the back of the figure . . . looks near the waist as if it had been compressed by the stay'.

3. Referred to in Fisher

4. Referred to in Fisher

5. Quoted in Fisher

6. *Screen*, 16:3 (Autumn, 1975), 6–18

7. Berger, p.47

8. P.A. Lemoine, *Degas et son œuvre* (Paris, 1946–9), vol.I, p.107

9. Quoted in Warner, p.65

10. Quoted in Tickner, note 6

11. Adrienne Rich, *Of Woman Born: Motherhood as Experience and Institution* (London, 1977)

12. For a detailed discussion of this picture and its authorship see Mary D. Garrard in Broude and Garrard, pp.146–71

13. Clark, p.6

14. Quoted in Sandy Nairne, *State of the Art: Ideas and Images in the 1980s* (London, 1987), p.151

15. Tickner, p.239

16. Feminist Anthology Collective, *No Turning Back* (London, 1981), p.240

17. Carolee Schneeman, *Cézanne She was a Great Painter* (1975)

18. Lippard, p.125

19. Tickner, p.243

20. In *Carving, a traditional sculpture*, the American Eleanor Antin documented a ten-pound weight loss in 144 photographs of her nude body, showing it gradually acquiring the prescribed shape of social and sexual desirability.

21. Berger, p.46

22. Alexis Hunter interview by Caroline Osborne, *Feminist Review*, 18 (November 1984), 49

23. *Of Mutability: Helen Chadwick*, catalogue of ICA exhibition (London, 1986)

24. Boston Women's Health Collective (New York, 1973)

25. Rich, *op.cit.*, p.39

26. Susan Griffin, *Woman and Nature* (London, 1984), p.217

27. Sarah Jane Edge, 'Pandora's Box at Rochdale', *Aspects*, 28 (1984) n.p.

28. See the exhibition catalogue, *The Possibility for Love: Joe Gantz*, Galerie J. et J. Donguy (Paris, 1987)

29. John Yau, 'How We Live: The Paintings of Robert Birmelin, Eric Fischl and Ed Paschke', *Artforum* (April 1983), 65

30. 'A Mirror to Yourself: Helen Chadwick in interview with Tom Evans', *Creative Camera*, 6 (1986), 25

BIBLIOGRAPHY

JOHN BERGER, *Ways of Seeing* (London, 1972)

ROSEMARY BETTERTON (ed.), *Looking On: Femininity in the Visual Arts and Media* (London, 1987)

FRANCES BORZELLO, *The Artist's Model* (London, 1982)

NORMA BROUDE and MARY D. GARRARD (eds), *Feminism and Art History: Questioning the Litany* (New York, 1982)

KENNETH CLARK, *The Nude* (London, 1956)

CAROL DUNCAN, 'Virility and Domination in Early 20th-Century Vanguard Painting', *Artforum* (December 1973)

ELIZABETH FISHER, *Woman's Creation: Sexual Evolution and the Shaping of Society* (London, 1980)

FRANCIS FRASCINA and CHARLES HARRISON (eds), *Modern Art and Modernism: A Critical Anthology* (London and New York, 1982)

TAMAR GARB, 'Renoir and the Natural Woman', *The Oxford Journal* 8:2 (1985)

SARAH KENT and JACQUELINE MORREAU (eds), *Women's Images of Men* (London, 1985)

JULIA KRISTEVA, *Desire in Language: A Semiotic Approach to Literature and Art* (New York, 1986)

ANNETTE KUHN, *The Power of the Image: Essays on Representation and Sexuality* (London, 1985)

GERDA LERNER, *The Creation of Patriarchy* (Oxford, 1986)

LUCY R. LIPPARD, *From the Center: Feminist Essays on Women's Art* (New York, 1976)

LYNDA NEAD, 'Representation, Sexuality and the Female Nude', *Art History*, VI, 2 (June 1983), 227–36

LYNDA NEAD, 'Woman as Temptress: The Siren and the Mermaid in Victorian Painting', *Leeds Art Calendar*, 91 (1982) 5–20

LINDA NOCHLIN, *Women, Art, and Power and Other Essays* (New York, 1988)

SHERRY B. ORTNER, 'Is Female to Male as Nature is to Culture?', *Feminist Studies* (Fall, 1972)

ROSZIKA PARKER and GRISELDA POLLOCK, *Old Mistresses* (London, 1981)

ROSZIKA PARKER and GRISELDA POLLOCK (eds), *Framing Feminism: Art and the Women's Movement 1970–1985* (London, 1987)

SUSAN RUBIN SULEIMAN (ed.), *The Female Body in Western Culture: Contemporary Perspectives* (Cambridge, Mass, and London, 1985)

LISA TICKNER, 'The Body Politic: Female Sexuality and Women Artists since 1970', *Art History*, I, 2 (June 1978)

MARGARET WALTERS, *The Nude Male* (London, 1978)

MARINA WARNER, *Monuments and Maidens: The Allegory of the Female Form* (London, 1985)

INDEX OF ARTISTS

Italic numerals refer to pages on which illustrations appear.

Agricola, Filippo *66*
Alberti, Leon Battista 17
Arrowsmith, Sue 130, 132, *139*
Arbus, Diane *8*

Baldry, Alfred Lys 94, *103*
Bandinelli, Baccio *51*
Barry, James 24
Bellmer, Hans 73
Bellocq, E.J. *47, 85*
Benglis, Lynda 118
Blake, William *33*, 129
Bloemaert, Frederick *19*
Botticelli, Sandro 10
Boucher, François 24, 99
Brandt, Bill 71, *76*, 86, *87*, 94, 100, *101*
Brassai *2*, 94, *100, 112*
Bravo, Manuel Alvarez *41*
Brigman, Annie W. *97*
Brodzky, Horace 75, *78, 84*
Burne-Jones, Sir Edward 95

Camp, Jeffery *127*, 129
Cézanne, Paul 93, 95
Chadwick, Helen 122, 123, *125*, 132, *136*
Chicago, Judy 120
Clausen, Sir George 75, *83*
Cooper, Eileen 123, *126*, 132, *137*
Coplans, John 130
Courbet, Gustave 72, 93, 95, 109, *110*
Cranach, Lucas 72

Degas, Edgar 25, *48, 53*
Dennett, Terry 94, *105*
Dossi, Dosso *69*

Dubuffet, Jean 74
Dürer, Albrecht 22, *30*, 71, 113

Earlom, Richard *133*
Etty, William 10, 93, *98, 99*

Fiedler, Franz *111*
Fischl, Eric 131
Floris, Frans 24, *32*, 33
Foster, F. *36*
Freud, Lucian 10, *16*
Frost 10
Fuseli, Henri *31*

Gantz, Joe 130, 131
Garrard, Rose 121, *135*
Gaudier-Brzeska, Henri *48*
Gauguin, Paul 93
Gentileschi, Artemisia 116
Gill, Eric *44*, 75, *78*
Giorgione 24, *40*, 93, 94, *106*
Giovane, Palma *67*
Goltzius, Hendrik *19*
Graham, Roberta 124, 129, *138*

Hardie, Gwen 123, 124, *127*, 132
Hepworth, Barbara *49*, 123
Hiller, Susan 121, *133*
Hilton, Roger *80*
Hunter, Alexis 120, 124, *128*

Ingres, Jean-Auguste-Dominique 24, *40*, 95, *115*

John, Gwen 109

Jones, Allen 38, 72, 73, *89*

Kauffmann, Angelica 116
Kelly, Mary 93, 117, 132
Kertesz, André 74, *90*
Kiff, Ken *54*
Klein, Yves 86
Klimt, Gustav 29, *42, 43*
Kooning, Willem de 73, 74

Lategan, Barry 121
Léger, Fernand *44*
Legros, Alphonse 93, *104*
Leighton, Frederic, Lord *57*
Lemoyne, François *37*
Leonardo da Vinci 10
Lommelin, A *36*
Luti, Benedetto *64*

Maes, Nicolaes *63*
Manet, Édouard 25, 94, *108*
Mapplethorpe, Robert 70, 71, 72
Masaccio 9, *12*
Matisse, Henri 39, *41*, 73, 93, *112*
McComb, Leonard 121
Medley, Robert 56
Michelangelo 18, 20, 28, 67
Millais, Sir John Everett 95, *114*
Millet, Jean-François 93, *97*
Moore, Henry *46*
Morreau, Jacqueline 124
Moser, Mary 116
Mulready, William 10, 18, *44*
Munch, Edvard 29, *70, 79*, 89
Muybridge, Eadweard *58, 59*

Opie, John *50*
Orpen, Sir William *108*

Parentino, Bernardo 18, *19*
Philpot, Glyn Warren *84*
Picasso, Pablo 73, 74, *90, 107*, 109,
    111, 113
Poussin, Nicolas 68

Poynter, Sir Edward John *52, 82*
Pruna, Pedro *86*

Raphael 32, 33, 36
Rea, Cecil 24
Rejlander, Oscar 29
Rembrandt van Rijn 28
Renoir, Pierre-Auguste 93, 95, *104*, 109
Reynolds, Sir Joshua 17, 18, 93
Ricketts, Charles *65*
Rodin, Auguste *109*
Rubens, Sir Peter Paul 7, *13, 35*, 36, 72

Salle, David 131
Sassetta, Stefano de Giovanni *14*
Sato, Hiro 97
Schmidt-Rottluff, Karl *109*
Schneeman, Carolee 118
Self, Colin *86*
Spence, Jo 94, *105*, 132
Spencer, Stanley 130
Stezaker, John 131
Stothard, Thomas *65*

Taraval, Jean Hughes *61*
Tenniel, Sir John *39*
Tintoretto, Jacopo 20, *34*, 45, *60*
Titian 10, 45, 46

Vaga, Perino del (school of) *20*
Van Gogh, Vincent 28, 95
Van Loo, Carle *62*
Vasari, Giorgio 18
Velasquez, Diego 45
Vouet, Simon *96*

Watson *45*
Wesselmann, Tom 73, *81, 88*
West, Benjamin 17, 22, 25, 26
Weston, Edward 94, *102, 103*
Williams, Andrew 121, *134*

Zoffany, Johann 116, 133
Zuccarelli, Francesco 24, *47*